ROC   E

DUST STORM

Stephen R. DeArman

outskirtspress
DENVER, COLORADO

This is a work of fiction. The events and characters described herein are imaginary and are not intended to refer to specific places or living persons. The opinions expressed in this manuscript are solely the opinions of the author and do not represent the opinions or thoughts of the publisher. The author has represented and warranted full ownership and/or legal right to publish all the materials in this book.

Rocket Babe
Dust Storm
All Rights Reserved.
Copyright © 2014 Stephen R. DeArman
v2.0 r1.0

Cover Photo © 2014 JupiterImages Corporation. All rights reserved - used with permission.
Interior Images: Stephen R. DeArman

This book may not be reproduced, transmitted, or stored in whole or in part by any means, including graphic, electronic, or mechanical without the express written consent of the publisher except in the case of brief quotations embodied in critical articles and reviews.

Outskirts Press, Inc.
http://www.outskirtspress.com

ISBN: 978-1-4787-2514-5

Outskirts Press and the "OP" logo are trademarks belonging to Outskirts Press, Inc.

PRINTED IN THE UNITED STATES OF AMERICA

Dedication

*For Verna, the love of my life, my greatest blessing,
and in every way, my Rocket Babe.*

*For my father; teacher, patriot, perfect role model
and first everlasting, best friend.*

*For my mother, children, and friends that have endured
a lifetime of my endless love of space, rockets and science fiction.*

*For all those men and women who have ridden the controlled explosion
we call rockets into space and for those who love and admire them.*

Acknowledgements

While this book is the result of a lifetime of personal education, experience and the intangible factor that I refer to as the scrapbook of my memory, the following people have greatly helped in the production of Rocket Babe.

Sharon Coffman, one of my dearest friends since first grade, without whose help this book would never have been completed. Sharon is an encourager, articulate and thorough, and I greatly enjoyed working with her.

Blake Driskill, our very good friend and "go to" man for all of our technology work.

David Miller, owner of Sirius Rocketry at http://www.siriusrocketry.com for allowing us to use his name and products in our story.

Rolf Stabroth, http://www.rolfstabroth.de World Class rocketeer and our very good friend in Germany.

Last but not least, *Mike Knowles*. The only person I ever knew who loved astronomy, space and science fiction as much as I do. He was a friend who passed much too early but will never be forgotten.

Prologue

As the supreme life form in the solar system, they had been visiting Earth with impunity for almost 1,000 years, all the while performing experiments on every form of life they encountered, mostly humans. And for all the time they had been observing human evolution and development they had done so without fear that one day man would dare challenge the very creatures that had tortured and used him like a lab rat. But now that day was dawning.

Occasionally visiting the air battles of World War II, their vehicles danced around the dogfights of mere humans, taunting the various militaries of Earth and allowing man to see flashes of their technological superiority. But man was advancing and would soon be going into space. The secret evil that had ruled the skies of this planet for so long would soon be directly challenged by man, but for humans to defeat them would require the bravest, strongest and most intelligent men and women mankind had to offer.

In the early 1960's the United States emerged as the nation that would lead the way to the moon and beyond and the fate of mankind would rest in the hands of the pilots, engineers, scientists and crewmen that would be sent into space to defend not just the U.S. but the planet.

While there were many brave men and women that would answer the call to duty, there was only one *Rocket Babe*.

Chapter 1

For NASA and earth bound scientists the Apollo missions had been very successful. The technological developments, experiments performed, samples and data collected would keep scientists occupied for years to come... and their military counterparts awake at night for much longer. As far as the world and general public knew, Apollo had been about winning the Space Race, but the real reason for going to the moon was not about one small step for man or beating the Russians to the punch. It was about determining if there could be life some place other than earth and not in a galaxy far, far, away but much closer to home. And it was also about developing the military capability to deal with extraterrestrial life should it prove to be something other than peaceful.

From ancient times the historical records of many cultures mentioned strange objects in the sky. As man moved into the 20th Century the reports of such objects increased at the same rate that human flight capabilities increased. During WW II some people called the objects Foo Fighters or flying saucers, but in the late 1950's, "UFO" became the permanent descriptive term. By the early 1960's human flight capabilities had progressed to the point that manned space flight was becoming a reality and a series of probes were sent to the moon. The first series of probes launched by the U.S. were called Ranger and among the thousands of photos sent back there had been many strange anomalies. Also strange was that many of the probes of the series seemed to malfunction frequently for no apparent reason. A few probes simply shutdown; others missed the moon entirely or crashed. Many scientists chalked it all up to a fledgling space agency "learning the ropes" of space flight, but for the privileged few of the inner circle of the U.S.

government there were other theories.

On June 2, 1966, the first of a series of soft landers called Surveyor began landing on the moon. Shortly after Surveyor 1 touched down in the southwest region of Oceanus Procellarum, NASA and the Pentagon knew there was more "up there" than could be seen from this planet. The Surveyor landers had two official goals: to demonstrate the feasibility of manned lunar landings and to send back close-up photos of the areas already chosen as possible Apollo landing sites. There was however a third and unofficial goal. All of the Surveyor landers had high resolution cameras and radar that were to be used to scan Space directly above the moon for anything out of the ordinary, and over the next three years a network of landers reported many "incidents." Within 2 hours of landing and activation, Surveyor 1 had picked up several glints of light above the lunar surface, and before the first full day of operation had passed there was a three second video of what looked to be a large dark triangle as it sped directly over Surveyor 1.

On the third day there was another video of a distant "orb" that abruptly changed course at a severe angle and then came to a full stop as if hovering, and after 30 seconds or so the orb suddenly changed direction again and moved out of sight at tremendous speed.

Later the same day Surveyor 1 picked up what appeared to be several seconds of video of a small irregular shadow casting from behind the camera and the last images from the moon were of a shower of sparks, as suddenly and without explanation the lander went dark. Everything to that point had worked flawlessly. As everyone at JPL worked frantically to find the cause of the failure, they were able to confirm the lander had been performing well and was in full operation. A quick systems check confirmed there had not been any accidental signals to shut down the lander. Even after a thorough item by item check had been performed, no reason could be found as to why everything suddenly stopped. From a micro-meteor strike, to a power overload caused by a solar flare, to moon quakes, over the next few days several theories were suggested for the failure of Surveyor 1 and all were eventually eliminated. NASA simply had no answer that made sense. But in an early morning meeting the following day the project manager finally made the one suggestion no one else was willing to make. He said, "Gentlemen, we have exhausted all possibilities except the one no one wants to state, but after reviewing the tapes and eliminating all known possibilities of normal operations and conditions we can only come to one conclusion: someone or something on the moon intentionally terminated the lander."

It was astounding but in the end it was the only possible explanation and at that point, NASA and the Apollo Program took on a new mission…

The actual space-to-ground audio tapes from NASA Archives July 20, 1969…

EAGLE: 540 feet, down at 30 [feet per second]…down at 15…400 feet down at 9…forward…350 feet, down at 4…300 feet, down 3 1/2…47 forward…1 1/2 down…13 forward…11 forward? coming down nicely…200 feet, 4 1/2 down…5 1/2 down…5 percent…75 feet…6 forward…lights on…down 2 1/2…40 feet? down 2 1/2, kicking up some dust…30 feet, 2 1/2 down…faint shadow…4 forward…4 forward…drifting to right a little…O.K.…

HOUSTON: 30 seconds [fuel remaining].

EAGLE: Contact light! O.K., engine stop…descent engine command override off…

HOUSTON: We copy you down, Eagle.

EAGLE: Houston, Tranquility Base here. The Eagle has landed!

HOUSTON: Roger, Tranquility. We copy you on the ground. You've got a bunch of guys about to turn blue. We're breathing again. Thanks a lot.

TRANQUILITY: Thank you…That may have seemed like a very long final phase. The auto targeting was taking us right into a football-field-sized crater, with a large number of big boulders and rocks for about one or two crater-diameters around it, and it required flying manually over the rock field to find a reasonably good area.

HOUSTON: Roger, we copy. It was beautiful from here, Tranquility. Over.

TRANQUILITY: We'll get to the details of what's around here, but it looks like a collection of just about every variety of shape, angularity, granularity, about every variety of rock you could find.

HOUSTON: Roger, Tranquility. Be advised there's lots of smiling faces in this room, and all over the world.

TRANQUILITY: There are two of them up here.

COLUMBIA: And don't forget one in the command module. End open transmissions…

As far anyone listening to the exchange outside of NASA knew, the time that lapsed between touchdown and man's first steps on the moon was spent performing system checks and getting ready for an historic EVA, but what actually transpired during that time was known only to the President, the participants, and a very small group of men at the Pentagon.

Finally on the surface and maintaining radio silence, two brave astronauts opened the forward hatch and prepared to perform a mission within the mission. They had been allotted 4 hours to get to the Ranger 8 crash site and back but walking on the surface was easier than had been expected. They bounced along at a good clip. In just under 20 minutes they were closing in on their target and the answer to some very important questions. Neither astronaut had spoken a word since leaving the LEM but as they arrived at their destination they could hardly contain themselves. For a few moments they stood trying to process what they were seeing, but soon they were back inside Tranquility Base preparing for their historical broadcast to Earth.

Breaking radio silence on a secured Pentagon channel only 2 hours later…

TRANQUILITY: Houston, Tranquility Base. L.G.M acquisition successful.

HOUSTON: Tranquility we copy L.G.M acquisition. The President says great job guys! Take a short break and prepare for the "official" first step onto the lunar surface.

TRANQUILITY: Roger Houston, we are GO for EVA.

A little over an hour later the world saw Neil Armstrong climb down a ladder onto the lunar surface for the first time… "That's one small step for man, one giant leap for mankind." Time stood still as the world watched Armstrong and Aldrin walk on the moon gathering rocks and soil samples, and while they would be bringing back a few things back to earth, they also left two things for whoever might visit their landing site in the future. The first item was a plaque that read "We came in peace for all mankind" to indicate their exploration was indeed peaceful in nature. The other was an American flag, and the flag was a marker with a message: *You will be dealing with us now and we're coming.*

The Apollo Program began as a series of manned missions to explore different areas of the moon for scientific purposes, taking various measurements and collecting rock samples to return to Earth. At least that's what the rest of the planet believed. But what the astronauts found was much more than rocks, dust and impact sediment. What they found would challenge mankind as never before and the U.S. Government concluded the general population could not handle the truth, nor should the U.S. share any knowledge gained from Apollo with other governments; and to that end a massive cover up was devised. There was a great deal of disinformation put forth over the next 10 years and by every means possible, even going as far as to have Hollywood make a movie suggesting that NASA had staged it all in the Nevada desert.

Following confirmation that we are not alone in the universe, an all out effort was launched by the Pentagon to prepare for contact and possible confrontation with whoever or whatever had been visiting Earth and its moon, but it took a while to reach a consensus on which branch of the Armed Forces should lead the way. After much debate it was finally decided to put together an entirely new branch of service, formed from the elite members of the Air Force, Army, Navy and Marines, tasked specifically to handle Space based operations and warfare. The new branch was called the United States Space Defense Force or S.D.F. for short. It was to be a completely covert branch of the military, based and operating exclusively out of Area 51. Over the following decade the S.D.F. grew to more than 10,000 men and women and evolved into 2 divisions: Near Earth Defense and the Deep Space Strike Force.

In the mean time, the Apollo Program had continued and completed missions 11-17 as originally scheduled, performing both official and unofficial duties. Then, with six successful landings behind them and with extreme pressure from the Pentagon, it was decided to officially cancel the last three planned moon landings, supposedly to reduce the budget. At that point the public's attention would turn toward a new program, the Space Shuttle. While the Shuttle program got on track, a new but completely unknown branch of the Armed Services was left with a small inventory of proven space worthy hardware ready to be deployed. Fortunately for the Pentagon, over the previous 15 years the U.S. Space Program had established a network of contractors, companies and personnel geared toward space flight, which meant the infrastructure was already in place to take manned space flight to the next level. Plus, there were already a number of rockets capable of sending heavy hardware and supplies into space and many more advanced vehicles on the drawing board.

As the S.D.F. struggled to get off the ground, it quickly became obvious that while the U.S. was now clearly the leader in space exploration on this planet, it was ill prepared to respond to a serious extended threat from space. The S.D.F. however would have to respond as best it could, even if it meant existing technology would be pushed to the breaking point and, in some cases, invented in order to speed things along, as there would be little time for testing or training. Whatever was required would have to be deployed as rapidly as possible and tested in the field. Current vehicles and procedures would simply have to be adapted for the coming missions.

Soon S.D.F. was using a variety of medium and heavy lift rockets for the Near Earth Defense forces, while the entire launch packages formerly reserved for Apollo missions 18, 19 and 20 would be reassigned and become the first deep space vehicles of the Deep Space Strike Force. Already completed or in some stage of construction were five additional Saturn V rockets, command and service modules, lunar modules and lunar rovers, with new vehicles going into production almost daily.

As Apollo was winding down and the new shuttle program cranked up with its much smaller budget, the S.D.F. went into overdrive and without financial limits but having the budget and hardware to do the job was only half the battle. The other half would be training the personnel that would crew the ships needed to take the fight to any and all alien life forms wherever they existed. Crew selection and training proceeded at a blistering pace. In all there were 3,000 men and women chosen to compete for 99 positions aboard the first three warships to be built.

Applicants that excelled in class work were then put through every conceivable mental and physical extreme to prove their worth, with the top 120 trainees qualifying for 99 astronaut positions. It took 6 grueling months but for those that made it through it meant the opportunity of a lifetime… and possibly a very short life, as these graduates would routinely be working in a very lethal environment with no practical experience and little real time working knowledge.

Of all the men and women that had been accepted into S.D.F. only one woman made the preliminary crew roster of the Pandora, and from the front yard of her home deep in the piney woods of rural Alabama, S.D.F. fighter pilot Captain Verna Starr sat and watched her next duty station pass overhead as a brilliant white object quickly moving through the Big Dipper.

Having bumped Venus as the 3rd brightest object in the sky and nearing completion, the Juno Class warship, U.S.S. PANDORA, SCVN 21 was now visible even in daylight. Soon, with a little help from Columbia and Challenger, the largest and most recent spaceship ever built by man would be supplied and ready for her maiden voyage. Orbiting 250 miles overhead at the Alan Shepard Ship Yard, the Pandora was scheduled to be fully operational January 1, 1982, but with final dry dock testing now behind her, the ship would be ready for service almost 2 weeks ahead of schedule.

For anyone seeing the ship up close the Pandora would have looked very familiar. Basically she was a heavily modified Saturn V with several substantial changes. With most of its sections built on the ground and then launched to the Shepard Yard for final assembly, converting a Saturn V from a multistage boost vehicle to a complete warship took a great deal of original thinking, not to mention re-engineering. Over the previous three year period it had taken 15 Titan III and two Columbia launches to put the Pandora into orbit. Supplying the ship for its first mission took a half dozen more.

While the fuselage and basic exterior appearance of the ship was similar to that of a full stack Saturn V, it only took a glance to see the Pandora was not your "old man's" Saturn V Moon Rocket. The tiny Apollo capsule had been replaced by a Command Bridge that added a full 72 feet to the overall package, bringing its total length to 425 feet.

No longer a three stage booster, the base rocket had been converted into one very large single stage vehicle with two large lander bays on either side of what would have normally been the first stage. The bays would serve double duty as launch and recovery ports for six armed lander/fighters, three per wing, re-designated as Vindicator, as well as provide the extra space needed for fighter pilots and support crew living quarters. One of the more innovative features of the bays were the two inch thick shatter proof retractable transparent doors that provided the ability to pressurize individual compartments. Pressurized compartments meant the flight crews would be much more efficient since they would not need space suits to perform routine duties and maintenance.

On the opposite end, the bridge looked kind of like the love child of a "Dyna-Soar" meets the Ascent Stage of the LEM (Lunar Excursion Module). Dubbed Cestris by the Black Ops firm Sirius that built it, the bridge provided three decks in all, two forward and one lower, aft. The main forward deck provided seating and operations stations for the pilot and copilot, radar operator, weapons officer, fire control, communication, Commander and XO. The secondary forward deck below provided five work stations for ship operations. The aft deck was below the main tube and housed most of the electronics, as well as provided crew quarters for 15.

The entire interior of the ship had been heavily modified and fortified as needed to withstand the additional stresses of a launch in space and extended high speed flight and braking. Every cubic inch in all three stages was used to power the ship or make room for additional crew and supplies. While the first stage was mostly a standard issue Saturn V booster with the usual five F1 engines, one third of the compartment's exterior was enclosed by a pair of cargo bay doors that fully opened to allow a small remotely controlled arm to quickly exchange and handle prefilled modular tanks for refueling or supply pods.

The second stage had been through a major internal overhaul as well. All five engines and their hardware had been removed in order to provide room for crew quarters and a pair of radioisotope thermoelectric generators (RTG) to power the ship and extended mission supplies.

In order to provide easy emergency access to any section of the ship, in addition to a heavy duty infrastructure, a continuous pressurized tube was installed along the port side of the hull that ran from stem to stern. The crew quarters and all human necessities were housed wherever the crew served aboard ship. The Vindicator pilots and their service quarters were aft by the lander bays, Marine and Ranger quarters were in what used to be the second stage, leaving the third stage for the command and bridge crew.

Because the Pandora was essentially a large single stage vehicle and already in space, the launch parameters would be somewhat different from those of a ground based launch, one bonus being that it would allow the engineers to replace the normal ullage rockets with eight megaton tactical nukes, giving the Pandora a total of four ground penetrating nuclear bombs and six strategic nuclear missiles. Aft, each wing had two sets of recessed twin 50 mm electric cannons, top and bottom side. In addition to the same cannon set up, the bridge also housed four Sidewinder, four Sparrow and two Phoenix Missiles.

The Pandora crew would consist of 33 handpicked officers and enlisted personnel: commander, lieutenant commander, chief medical officer, CAG, command pilot, co-pilot, chief engineer, communications officer, flight engineer, six combat pilots, six marines, six rangers and six enlisted Air Force personnel.

By no coincidence the SDF was 98% male, so for that day and age being chosen to serve aboard the Pandora was an historical achievement for a woman. But Verna was not merely the youngest woman to serve in the Space Defense Force, she was the only woman serving in the Deep Space Strike Force. While there had been thousands of applicants, male and female, only the top one percent made the cut for the DSSF and of that one percent, Verna was the only woman to make the roster of the Pandora.

As Verna went back into the house her thoughts were on the coming mission to Mars. It seemed her entire life had been destined for this moment and mission. All of her education, all of her training, everything she had ever accomplished and worked for had led her to the DSSF and now it was time to put it all to work. She was mentally and physically prepared for anything and everything that was to come and she drifted off to sleep anxious to go to Mars.

Chapter 2

On the morning of December 1, 1981, Pandora's newly assigned Commanding Officer, Carl J. Jackson, was going over the ship's duty roster with his Executive Officer, Lt. Commander William Collins, when about half way down the spreadsheet he came across what he thought must certainly be a misprint. After a moment he looked at his XO and asked him, "Is that a woman's name I see?"

"Looks like it, sir."

"No way, Bill! It must be a typo; probably should have been Vernon Starr, or something like that."

"No sir; no typo. She's a woman sir; all woman. I've met her."

"Are you serious? A woman pilot? Assigned to my ship?"

"Yes, sir, and a great one at that. I'm surprised you haven't heard of her, sir."

"Well, Mr. Collins, until this moment, I was blissfully unaware of her existence, but since you seem to know so much, perhaps you will enlighten me. Give me one good reason why I shouldn't have her removed from the roster immediately. You know as well as I do that technically none of us are qualified to go on this mission. It will be the longest, most dangerous expedition any group of men has ever attempted; requiring the absolute best man there is available at every position. There's no way a woman will be able to handle it."

Having worked with Commander Jackson for some time now and knowing he demanded perfection from everyone under his command, Collins smiled and said, "That's what you have on the roster, the absolute best personnel. But tell me sir, how long do you have and how much would you like to know about Starr? It could take a while but I can tell you this right now, there are many reasons you want her on board the Pandora and you definitely do not want to request her removal from the crew. I can share her dossier, family, and personal background, or my personal experiences with her. So what would you like to hear first?"

Commander Jackson thought for a moment and then said, "Just start talking Bill; I'll tell you when to stop."

"Yes sir. Let's start by getting the formal information out of the way. Her name is Verna Louise Starr, Captain, USAF, F-16 interceptor pilot. She currently holds the highest proficiency rating in USAF in all flight categories; extremely gifted mentally, athletically, and academically. She has an estimated I.Q. of 195+.

"Her intelligence and eidetic memory placed her at the top of her classes all the way through school including the Air Force Academy. By the age of 20, she had obtained her BS, a Masters of Astrophysics, and was serving in the U.S. Air Force as an interceptor pilot at Homestead Air Force Base. She has won numerous awards and commendations for air combat skills and her number of kills, both in training simulations and live action. Recommendation to NASA came from several superior officers and the base Commander at Homestead. Even though her credentials and accomplishments are impressive, her recommendation for service on the Pandora came after she saved her Vindicator flight instructor and herself when he had a heart attack during a training flight. By performing several maneuvers that exceeded the space craft's design, she manually landed her Vindicator on the main flight deck of the Shepard Yard five minutes ahead of normal automatic procedures. That five minutes made the difference in quickly getting the medical help her instructor needed and saved his life, her life, and a multimillion dollar space craft. For her actions that day she was awarded the Air Force Cross. Soon after, she was offered the opportunity to transfer to DSSF where she qualified for the last available fighter pilot position aboard the Pandora. Shall I go on sir?"

Again Commander Jackson paused a moment before answering.

"So, what you're describing here, Bill… is a real live human Mr. Spock?"

"Not exactly sir; more like Mr. Spock's younger sister."

Laughing sarcastically Jackson said, "Then I suppose she must actually be from Vulcan, right?"

"Not quite, sir, although there is a large cast iron statute of Vulcan near her home. She was born, raised, and except for the Academy, she was educated in Alabama. Hence her predilection for crimson and white, but the comparison to the mythical TV character is accurate. She would easily be the most intelligent person onboard Pandora."

Jackson smiled and said, "I'm not sure I like the idea of a subordinate being smarter than me, especially if they happen to be a woman."

Collins grinned at him. "You know, Carl, like Mr. Dylan says, 'The times they are a changing.'"

"Marshall Dillon said that?"

"No, Bob Dylan. There will soon come a day when women are going to be as much a part of things as men."

"Perhaps, my old friend, but not today. And let's hope I'm dead and gone before we see that happen in DSSF. Our fathers blew it when they gave them the right to vote. They should have kept them barefoot and pregnant."

"Spoken like a true chauvinist, Carl."

"Thank you, Bill, but there's no need for flattery. Your position as XO is safe as long as I'm in command."

"That's good to know, sir. I'm sure to sleep better on the mission knowing I'll get to stand next to you when it all hits the fan."

"Ok, let's get back to Starr. That's all very impressive, Bill, but I didn't hear anything that makes me comfortable about taking a young woman to Mars, especially when every move we make could be our last." Then picking up the phone he began dialing, saying, "No, no, I think I'll be calling the Pentagon right now about exchanging her for a more experienced replacement." Collins began to tell him it would require too much paper work and then he tried to explain her appointment further, but Commander Jackson cut him off.

With Jackson motioning for Collins to be quiet while he made the call, Collins tried one last time to explain and said, "Seriously sir, I wouldn't do that."

"Really? YOU wouldn't do that?"

"No, sir, I would not. You see, sir, the man that recommended her for the Pandora was..." but Collins was cut off as Commander Jackson turned his back on him. Quietly Collins muttered to himself, "Ok sir, I tried to warn you."

As Jackson heard the phone ringing on the other end, he pushed the speaker button on his phone so Collins could hear the conversation. "Now Bill, you can hear how it's done without all the usual red tape."

Grinning broadly at him Collins responded, "Oh, I'm all ears, sir."

The phone clicked and a voice answered, "DSSF, Captain Vincent speaking. How may I help you?"

"Captain, this is Commander Jackson, U.S.S. Pandora. I need to speak to the head of man power for DSSF."

"Yes, sir. Just a moment, Commander."

A few seconds later a gravelly voice answered, "Colonel Anderson here."

"Colonel, this is Commander Jackson, U.S.S. Pandora. I believe there's been a major mistake on my ship's duty roster and I need to request an immediate personnel change."

"What mistake would that be, Commander?"

"Well, Colonel, it seems that somehow a woman has been assigned to my ship and I need to get that corrected ASAP. Jackson smiled smugly and glanced at Collins to see that he was also smiling as he listened to the conversation.

"Commander, are you referring to Captain Starr?"

"Yes, that's right! Captain Starr! I take it you're familiar with her, Colonel. I'm sure she's quite the little pilot but I believe I need a more qualified *man* to replace her…" and then for emphasis Jackson raised his voice and emphatically said, "…and I need one now!"

Trying not to laugh out loud at the demand, Anderson paused a moment before answering, "I'm sorry, Commander Jackson, but I'm afraid that just won't be possible."

"Really? Why is that Colonel? Are you in charge of personnel or not? Maybe I need to speak to your superior!"

After a brief moment Colonel Anderson asked, "Would you like to speak to my superior, Commander?"

"Absolutely! Get him on the phone. Right now!"

Commander Jackson looked at Collins to see him now cringing and shaking his head side to side as Jackson made the request, but at that moment they heard the Colonel say, "Just a moment, Commander. I'll be more than happy to connect you."

As his words came back over the phone, Commander Jackson smiled and told Collins, "You see, Bill, you just have to be firm with these bean counters. Now watch and learn."

"Oh, yes sir, I'm watching," Collins said, suppressing his own laughter.

Again the phone clicked and this time they could hear, "Office of the President, Secretary Jane Lawson speaking. How may I assist you?"

"Miss Lawson, this is Colonel Anderson. Commander Jackson of the U.S.S. Pandora would like to speak with the President, please."

As the Colonel's words echoed over the line, Collins could see the color begin to drain from Commander Jackson's face. "Just a moment, Colonel. I believe the President is available." Jackson scowled and quickly looked at Collins, who was trying hard not to laugh out loud. Then before he could think of some way to get out of the call he heard the President on the line.

"This is the President, Commander Jackson. How can I help you today?"

The rapid turn of events had stunned Jackson for a moment and he hesitated at first. After a long pause the President said, "Hello, are you there?"

Jackson finally spoke up and said, "Yes sir. Good day, sir. The reason I'm calling is that I was just going over the duty roster for the Pandora with Lt. Commander Collins and I saw a listing for a young woman, a Captain Starr."

"Oh yes," the president interrupted. "I know Bill Collins well. He'll be a great second in command for you and yes, I know Captain Starr, too. A fine girl; fine girl! She saved my nephew Ben's life a while back, you know. I'm sure she'll make you a fine pilot."

"Well... yes, sir. That's why I'm calling, to say... thank you, for the recommendation."

"Ohhh, you're welcome Commander, but you didn't need to call and thank me personally. We'll do anything for our brave men and women in space. I'm looking forward to seeing you launch next month, on the QT of course."

"Yes sir, of course. Uh... thank you again, sir."

"Well, you're quite welcome, Commander, and if there's anything you or the crew needs just let me know. Listen, I hate to be short, Commander, but I've got to go now. Maggie is waiting in the Rose Garden. Thanks again for calling. Goodbye!"

As the phone disconnected and they were left with only a loud dial tone, Collins began laughing hysterically. Actually, it was more like a howl than laughter. Commander Jackson stood there looking stunned as Collins tried to collect himself. As his mind began to function again he looked at Collins and said, "So... the man she saved that had the heart attack in space while she was completing her Vindicator flight training was the President's nephew?"

Collins tried to stop laughing and confirmed his statement, "Yes, sir."

"And she was put up for DSSF by the President himself?"

"Yes sir, that's correct. Any more questions?"

After a few moments Jackson said, "I hope you're enjoying yourself, Bill. You could have warned me."

"I tried to, Carl, but you said you knew how to handle these 'bean counters,' so...."

Jackson now looked more than a little upset and asked, "Bill, how would you like to be reassigned to the aft sensor section all the way to Mars?"

"Who, me? No sir! I'm sorry sir; won't happen again, sir!"

"Bill, I don't care what the President says. I still have concerns about her serving on the Pandora. I want to know more about her. What's your relationship to Starr?"

"Well sir, I had been stationed at Homestead for several years when she was first assigned there as an interceptor pilot, and I spent several months flying all kinds of training missions with her, from air to air refueling, to any number of combat roles and head to head."

"How did she do with you?"

"Initially she defeated me, sir, three out of three rounds, but over a six week period she defeated me six out of six."

"Really? Six out of six?" Jackson asked in amazement. "I thought you were a triple ace. Is she that good?"

"I am, and yes sir, she's that good. I thought I had her cold on two different engagements when she baited me into some form of twisted Pugachev's Cobra the first time, and again when she used some kind of ninja type J turn. Neither of which should have been possible with the aircraft she was flying at the time. I'm still not exactly sure how she pulled off either maneuver without vectored thrust. I mean, it was almost like she was flying a hummingbird."

"Did you ever ask her where she learned such a maneuver?"

"Yes, sir, I did. All she said was an old family friend named Rollie that works for some place called *Sirius*."

"Do you know of a simulator that she could have practiced her 'ninja skills' on?"

"No, sir. A simulation like that is still on the drawing boards, along with the aircraft that is designed to perform such a maneuver. And there was one other incident. I didn't see it, but an old Viet Nam buddy of mine told me that on his engagement with her she used a maneuver on him that he could only describe as a 'forward spin,' almost like a pin wheel, but he wouldn't talk about it after his original debriefing because they all said he was flying drunk or just made it up when he lost to a female. When I talked to him about it all he would say is that the maneuver he saw should only have been possible if you were a flying a spacecraft with thrusters all over it."

"What were they flying, Bill?"

"He was in a Tomcat and she was flying her Falcon."

"Hmmm. Ok, go on with your story."

"Several months before all of this happened she got her first big break, when by luck or by fate she came at just the right time to be involved in a very nasty exchange with the Cubans that was never publicized. Do you remember some unofficial backroom intel about four MiGs going down in the Gulf a couple of years back?"

"Yes, I heard something about that. I believe that was when a pair of F-16's took down four MiGs in less than five minutes."

"Yes, sir, but it was more like Starr took down three of them, and she was a rookie wingman only three weeks into her first assignment."

Commander Jackson leaned back in his chair and seemed to be deep in thought. After a minute or so he looked at Collins and said, "Bill, get me all her files and the contact information for her squadron leader at Homestead. I want to speak to him."

Chapter 3

Three days later a large folder with Captain Starr's complete service record arrived on Commander Jackson's desk labeled TOP SECRET. He had never seen any pilot's personnel folder labeled as such and it made him all the more curious about Captain Starr. Before he realized it he had spent the better part of the day reading report after glowing report of her classroom successes and aerial exploits. What impressed him the most was that without exception, Starr had been recommended for astronaut training by every instructor and squadron leader she had ever served with, not to mention a very high recommendation from the Commander In Chief himself.

By the time he was finished with her file Jackson was almost ready to start believing that maybe this woman could be as good as advertised, but he just couldn't shake the feeling that it was all just a little too good to be true. She must be as close to perfect as a human could get but there had to be a flaw some place. Before they launched for Mars he wanted to know what that flaw might be, but all Jackson could find was that from day one her school records were perfect; all top of the class. Her parents were simple people from the quiet country town of Altoona; her mom a school teacher, her dad a fireman. She was an only child but with many friends, all of whom spoke very highly of her as well. Her flight qualifications were extremely impressive and over the last five years she had logged many hours piloting numerous fighters including the F-104 Starfighter, F-105 Thunderchief, F-106 Delta Dart, F-4 Phantom II, A-4 Skyhawk, F-15 Eagle and F-16 jet fighters, as well as a few hops as copilot on a B-52 and a SR-71.

Finally convinced of her accomplishments to date and skills as a pilot, Commander Jackson moved on to the most referenced pilot in her file, her first Squadron Leader, Major Samuel Norris, aka *Sidewinder*. Jackson decided to call Homestead only to find Norris had retired. Not to be dissuaded, he had Collins locate Norris for him. After a brief discussion with Collins, Norris reluctantly agreed to meet with Jackson. Early the next day the Commander flew to Miami for the meeting. A short drive from the airport brought Jackson to an old shack on the southern edge of the Everglades where he found Norris enjoying his breakfast and sitting under a large palm tree sipping a Corona. Nailed to the tree was a thermometer that indicated 91 °F and below it was a clock that read 9:33.

Jackson walked up to Norris, put out his hand and asked, "Major Norris?"

"Nope, just plain Sam," was the answer as Norris shook his hand. "Major Norris has left the building. Or you could call me Sidewinder; most people do. I take it you're Commander Jackson. Would you like a Corona, Commander?"

"I don't think so; it's a little early for me."

"Suit yourself, Commander. What brings you to sunny Florida on such a warm day?"

"I'd like to talk to you about Air Force Captain Verna Starr."

"So… you want to talk about Rookie. How's she doing? Is she still flying all the aces out of their seats?"

"Well, sort of. At the moment she's learning to fly in space."

Norris didn't want to spend the day beating around the bush so he looked Commander Jackson squarely in the eyes and said, "Commander, I'm sure you're a busy man and I prefer to shoot straight, so let's drop all the formalities and pretense and get to the point. I'm pretty sure you have Rookie's files, so let's save some time and get down to why you're really here."

"Good," Jackson replied, "I like that; right to the point. Here it is… I assume you know that when Captain Starr left Homestead she went to Houston for astronaut training."

"Yep, I know. I was the one that recommended her for it, but you knew that already... Boy! You should have seen her exit."

"Well, recently she was assigned to me as a pilot and I'm not sure she's up to the task."

At hearing that, Norris spewed a pint of beer and laughed loudly. "Rookie? Not up to it? That's a hoot Commander. Tell me, how long have you known her?"

"Not long at all. That is, she hasn't reported to me yet. I only know what's in her file and some scuttle butt from other pilots. What I want to know is what isn't in the file and since you flew with her the longest and were the closest pilot to her, I'd like your professional opinion on her abilities. I'm sure you'd agree that they can't put everything there is to know about a pilot's abilities in a file."

Suddenly Norris sat straight up and his tone turned angry. "I'm not sure what you're driving at Commander, but if you think she isn't up to ANY task you might have for her, you need to think again. She'll out-think, out-fly, out-work and out-last anyone under your command, including you. Test her. She'll make you look like a fool. If you doubt her abilities, why don't you mount up and try her out one on one? I think I would enjoy watching that! Or have you been flying a desk too long?"

Seeing he was about to lose Norris's good will, Jackson paused a moment and tried to take a different angle. "Look Norris... Sam, I'm just trying to make sure she has what it takes to be under my command. Surely you can understand that. Being a pilot in space isn't like being a regular fighter pilot."

Norris leaned forward, almost nose to nose and snapped, "What I understand is that you don't want a female pilot on the Pandora."

A long pause followed as Jackson bristled at his statement and shot back, "How did you know she was assigned to the Pandora? How do you even know about the Pandora?"

Norris smiled and said, "I didn't spend 30 years in USAF and not pick up a few friends at higher levels. I know quite a bit about a couple of agencies that officially do not exist like… SDF and DSSF. But you know what I mean. I'm sure with the number of years you've put in, you have a few friends at the Pentagon, don't you commander?" Commander Jackson grinned a bit and nodded his head.

Norris looked at Jackson and asked, "Are you going to deny her what she's earned Commander?"

Wishing to relieve the rapidly rising tension between them Jackson quickly responded, "No, I've given up on that. I already tried to have her removed and found that her friends out rank mine. No, this is much simpler, Major. More than anyone referenced in her file, you've pushed her for promotion, written letters of recommendation like I've never read before, and I need to know why you are so impressed with her that she would merit a position, any position, on my ship."

"That will be easy, Commander. Let me tell you a little story about a rookie that came here a few years back, barely 21 and wet behind the ears. Back then I had the same attitude toward female pilots as you have now. I didn't agree with the idea of women being in USAF at all, much less as a fighter pilot and I sure as heck didn't want to nurse maid one through combat training. But so you'll understand why I changed my mind, here's the deal.

"Starr had only been at Homestead three weeks when she experienced her first enemy engagement. She was sipping a Kona coffee and sitting in the alert ready room monitoring tower chatter when Homestead radar picked up four aircraft coming out of Cuba and headed directly for the base at high speed. She and I were the pilots pulling alert duty that day, and she was my wingman. When she heard the tower report she instantly ran to her plane and climbed aboard.

"As we were strapping in, I glanced over at her to make sure she was ready to go. We had only spoken briefly a time or two in preflight meetings and she had never had to respond to a real threat. We had a surprise practice alert scheduled for her later that same day, but the real thing came along first. Just as the klaxon blared and Homestead went on full alert, a couple of airmen ran under our planes and pulled the chocks away and we rolled a pair of brand new F-16's out of the hangar, side by side. Then, as we started down the taxiway she comes over my headset, 'Is that you, Major Norris?' I responded, 'When we're in the air you call me Sidewinder, Rookie. And don't be scared, you just listen to me and I'll get your butt back to base, got it?' 'Scared!' she comes back at me. 'Who's scared? I just want to know who I'm flying with. Don't *you* be scared Major. I can get my own butt back to base, sir.' Yeah, she was a little cocky; still blowin' and crappin' green, but I liked her spunk.

"Our canopies were still coming down when the radios crackled, 'Lightning Flight, you are cleared for takeoff,' and within seconds we're rolling down the main runway with afterburners blazing. After a couple hundred yards we lifted to 25 feet, retracted gears, and held there until we were almost to the end of the tarmac. Then I said, 'Time to climb, Rookie,' and with that we pulled back hard on the sticks and screamed almost straight up. To my amazement she maintained her position to the inch the entire way. No bobbing, no weaving, it was like she was part of my plane.

"In less than 60 seconds we were well over Mach 1, leveled off at 25,000 feet and closing on target. When I finally had visual contact I reported back to Homestead that we had four MiG-21's, Angels 25. This was not the first time MiGs from Cuba had threatened an attack on Homestead but they had always turned back before being directly confronted, and with a rookie along I was hoping this would just be another idle threat. With the MiGs refusing to respond to repeated requests by the Homestead tower to alter course, and being only 20 miles southwest of the base, we were ordered to engage the MiGs. And let me say here Commander: be careful what you say around her. She hears everything! Starr told me later that under my breath but over the comlink I mumbled something about going into combat with a 'damn rookie female wingman.' I came to regret that statement rather quickly.

"About that time I said, 'Rookie, we're going to fly high and wide as we pass them, then pivot into firing position.' I was thinking she's going to be flustered or scared and forget what to do but she was stone cold! Starr responded, 'Roger that, Sidewinder; maneuvering for W E Z.' As we approached the MiGs from a high 9 position, she crossed over my flight path from the rear in order to obtain a weapons engagement zone. Just as she obtained W E Z the MiGs broke formation with one pair attempting to turn back toward us, the other pair continuing on toward the base.

"Rookie became concerned and said, 'Sidewinder, they're trying to draw us off so the Castro Twins can go for the base!' I said, 'It appears that way, Rookie, but turning into our firing position is making this too easy.' Banking hard left I called out, 'I've got the one on the left. You take the one on the right.' But Rookie was way ahead of me and had already achieved a lock on her target. She instantly responded with, 'Roger right, FOX 2!' and got her shot off before the words were completely out of my mouth. I followed her AIM 7 Sparrow with one of my own. In just seconds the rockets found their targets and the first MiG burst into flames, then a second or so later the second MiG exploded and fell toward the Gulf. I notified Homestead we had splashed two, and while getting the first pair was great, we still had two more to deal with, so I told her to put her foot into it.

"Pulling almost eight G's, we banked hard and again went to full afterburners and I'm telling you having her for a wingman is like flying next to a mirror. She matches whatever you do like she's part of your aircraft. But just as we were coming out of the turn, my bird starts losing power and Starr glances over to see me slowing down and losing altitude. I told her I'd had a flame out and Rookie pulled back on her throttle, waiting to see if I could get a response from my bird. After several attempts to restart with no luck, and with precious seconds passing I finally told her, 'You're going to have to go for it Rookie. Splash the MiGs!' She wanted to know if I was going to be ok and I told her I'd be fine, just take down the MiGs! She quickly went to her afterburner in pursuit of her next target. I watched her head off after them and figured I'd never see her alive again."

You could tell the events of that day were worthy of the Commander's attention to detail. By her report, the Falcon had instantly responded to her demand for more speed and she rapidly closed on her targets. Pushing 900 knots, Starr watched for the display on her visor to indicate she had reached weapons range and prepared to fire. Then right on cue the targeting radar began its familiar whine. She maneuvered to get a lock on the trailing MiG, but just as she was about to fire, again they suddenly split up and were turning back toward her from opposing directions. Without hesitation she continued to close on the trailing MiG and got a good tone as he was about half way into his turn. Pushing the launch button, she watched the smoke trail of the Sparrow until it met the MiG just as he came out of the turn. There was a bright flash as the plane exploded, scattering him across the sky.

While she was taking out MiG number three, the remaining MiG had managed to maneuver to her left flank and was almost in firing position. Suddenly her alarm went off. MiG number four had a lock and was firing. As a Russian R-60 missile closed on her, she was forced to go totally evasive. First she dumped both chaff pods to put some extra heat in a different direction as she rolled hard right, then down at a severe angle. The Russian missile took the bait and the high G maneuver allowed her to duck back under its flight path. While all of this was going on MiG number four was doing its best to follow her erratic gyrations in order to maintain firing position.

All the abrupt turns and power dive had momentarily caused her to lose track of MiG number four, but she was quickly reminded of his position when her alarm went off and her bird was hit. Instinctively she went to full throttle and broke hard right and maintained the turn until she could see MiG number four trying to follow. A quick glance at her console showed all systems normal. Nothing critical had been hit but the MiG pilot was still trying to follow her lead. At that point she cracked a smile because she knew she had him if he continued to try and follow her turn.

Starr knew her F16 could turn inside the radius of any MiG if they stayed in a tight turn long enough, so that's what she decided to do. About 3/4 of the way through the first circle she had almost over taken him and was now coming up on his six. At that point the MiG pilot realized what was happening and decided to make a run for it. He broke left and began a flat out run for home but that was his last mistake.

The MiG tried to accelerate away from her but she over took him in short order. She said it would have been easy to back off and let him gain some distance before firing her last missile, but then she decided to save the tax payers a few dollars and use her guns. The MiG tried to evade her but she quickly had her guns aimed right up his exhaust and a quick tap on the trigger was all it took to shut him down. There was no need for a long burst. Bullets cost the tax payers too, according to Starr.

The commander continued, "Thick black smoke flowed from that doomed plane as it began to lose altitude. She backed off a bit and briefly followed along to see if the pilot would eject, but she didn't have to wait long for the answer. As expected, the canopy flipped up and off and was quickly followed by the pilot ejecting. As she saw his chute open she was thinking 'It's pretty cold at 25,000 feet and a long way to the Gulf below,' but then she remembered that by then I was probably in the Gulf too.'

"Even though she was low on fuel she wanted to join the search for me but she was ordered back to base. Not long after she landed, I was picked up and brought to the infirmary and our base Commander, Colonel Swanson, joined us. He was there to make sure all was well and when he asked her how she had managed it, she tried to give me all the credit. She said, 'Everything I did, I learned from Major Norris, sir.' Can you believe that? I hadn't taught her anything at that point. And for the next three weeks she took care of me whenever she wasn't flying. She changed bandages, cooked for me, and even took my clothes to the cleaners. You know, she says I remind her of Tommy Lee Jones. That's a hoot!

"Her success with the MiGs was the first indication of her true abilities but not the last. Not long after that, Colonel Swanson assigned me to help develop her skills and gain some experience. Over the next 12 months Rookie spent more time in the air than any other pilot in USAF. She qualified for every combat school available and she was gaining more knowledge and tactical skills than pilots twice her age and with many more years of service. In less than one year she had participated in all seven national combat competitions and achieved First Place, seven out of seven times. Her reputation as a pilot and her successes against the best the U.S. had to throw at her had not gone unnoticed, and soon she was approached by the top brass at the Pentagon about becoming an astronaut.

"So, did I recommend her for NASA? You bet, and I'm proud to have been the one. I knew we were losing a great fighter pilot but she was destined for much more than being a jet jockey. The day she left was about the saddest day of my life and I remember it well. It seemed just like any other Monday in sunny Florida when she walked into the alert ready room; that is until she saw me sitting at the Ops desk waiting for her. She snapped off her usual salute and said, 'Good morning sir!' I tried to look at her sternly for a moment and then said, 'It is a good morning, for you, Captain.' She said, 'How is that sir?' And I replied, 'Well Captain, it seems I have the honor of handing you your transfer papers.'

"She was startled at first, then managed to get out, '*Transfer papers*? I didn't request a transfer! What's going on sir? Why would they transfer me without notice? Did you ask for me to be transferred? I haven't done anything wrong.' I told her, 'Well, why don't you just read the letter Captain, and let's see what it's all about.'

"Starr took the letter from me, opened it with one quick motion and began reading it out loud. 'From the National Aeronautics Space Administration to Captain Verna L. Starr, USAF. Captain Starr, please report immediately to the Astronaut Training Facility, Johnson Space Center, Houston, Texas. Upon arrival, report to Captain Mike Knowles, Astronaut Training.'

"It was the only time I ever saw Rookie the least bit confused. 'What does it mean, sir?' I had worked my butt off getting her the recommendation so I was amused and a little proud too. I looked at her, laughed and said, what do you mean, 'what does it mean,' Rookie? I'd say it looks like you're going to be an astronaut! The very first female astronaut! She was actually stunned and sat down next to my desk. 'Me? Really? They want me?' Looks like it, and they want you there, today, I told her. 'Today? How can I be there today? We have a flight scheduled, I'm not packed; I don't have a way to get there… I have to call my parents!'

"I let her stew for a minute or two then I finally told her, 'Everything has already been arranged. We'll have your gear sent to you this afternoon on the next C-5 going to Houston. As for transportation, you are authorized to take your plane and turn it in to Major Brantley at Barksdale. He'll take you to Captain Knowles who will get you settled in.'

"Rookie was having a hard time taking it all in. She must have asked me three or four times if I really meant, 'right now!' I said, 'Yep, right now. Your plane is fueled and as soon as you can preflight you need to get in the air.' She was still in shock. 'This is happening too fast sir, I'm not prepared.' 'Well, you'll have about 90 minutes to prepare on your way, so let's get you prepped.' And in just a few minutes her Falcon was ready and burning fuel.

"I walked her to her plane and said, 'She's ready Captain; she's all yours... for the next 90 minutes.' She looked at me and said, 'You knew this was coming, didn't you, sir? You did this?' And I said, 'Yep! I'm the one whose neck is out there if you screw this up, Rookie, so don't screw this up.' She smiled and got her flight suit and helmet on and when she was finally ready to go she smiled at me again and stood ramrod straight with her finger tips to her temple. I snapped to attention and saluted back. 'Good luck, Captain.' 'Thank you, sir. Before I go, permission to speak off the record, sir?' 'Granted.' Then she stepped forward, kissed me on the cheek and said, 'Thank you, sir.' It kind of flustered me for a moment so I just told her to, 'Get your butt in the air, Rookie!' I'd never had a captain kiss me before and it never happened again.

"Then she climbed the ladder and closed the canopy as she rolled out the door for the last time. I had the tower hold her up long enough for us to give her a little send off out on the main runway. I mean they gave her the works too; kept her waiting for a while. I could hear the tower over my Jeep's radio as we waited for her, 'Homestead Tower, Falcon 2-7 requesting permission for takeoff.' 'Acknowledged Falcon 2-7; please hold.' She held on the end of the taxiway for what seemed like an eternity to her but nothing was moving, not a single plane. She didn't get it at first. Then... 'Falcon 2-7, proceed to runway niner.' It took a couple of minutes to get there but finally she turned out onto the numbers and held for final clearance. A little way up the runway she could see a vehicle with several people standing out near the side of the runway. 'Falcon 2-7 you are cleared for takeoff. Be aware of the activity by the edge of the runway at V-2.' 'Roger tower. Falcon 2-7 aware and departing.'

"Pushing it to full afterburner she began her roll and quickly lifted off the ground to 25 feet as usual. With her speed rapidly rising as she approached the group's position by the edge of the runway, she looked down to see me and most of the flight crew saluting as she went by.

As she got to our position she pulled back hard and climbed straight up. As soon as she had enough altitude she did a complete loop and came back over the runway right at our position with a deafening roar, before again climbing out of sight on her way to JSC. We stood there watching her for a moment then Colonel Swanson looked at me and said, 'Dad gum rookie; thinks she's in the Thunderbirds!'"

It had been a lot to take in but Commander Jackson was impressed by Norris's passion for his former student's abilities. Clearly he had tremendous faith in Captain Starr. "Thank you, Major, for the intel and your time. I only have one other question about Starr. I know she's very intelligent and well trained, but how do you think she has been so successful to this point, especially when flying against pilots with much more experience?"

Norris smiled and continued, "Well sir, over the last couple of years she's gained a lot of experience and I do know what gives her an edge but that's something, Commander, you'll have to discover on your own... if you can."

Commander Jackson walked to his car as Norris followed. "Here's the last thing I'm going to share with you, sir. You want to take her to Mars, because if you don't, there's a very good chance that neither you, nor your crew, will come back." Jackson grinned and nodded as he pulled away.

On the way back Jackson decided he had gathered all the information he could from other sources. It was time to speak to Starr personally and see once and for all if she was as intelligent and impressive as he had been led to believe.

Chapter 4

Commander Jackson arrived back at his office to find XO Collins hard at work arranging flights for the Pandora crew. Coming through the door Jackson asked, "How are things coming, Bill?"

"We're set, Commander. The entire crew will be at the Cape in two days and we're scheduled for our first official assembly at 1300 that day."

"Good. And when do you and I leave?"

"Our flight out is 1800 this evening, sir."

"That's excellent, Bill… and Starr?"

"She's already there, sir, and knows you want to meet with her tomorrow at 0900."

"Excellent! You know, I think I'm actually looking forward to it."

"Glad to hear that, sir. Was Major Norris able to put your concerns to rest?"

"Not exactly, but I should know everything I need to know by tomorrow night." Collins wasn't sure what that meant but decided not to inquire further.

At exactly 0900 the next morning Verna arrived at Commander Jackson's office and was warmly greeted by Collins. Upon seeing her he began smiling ear to ear and hugged her tightly. "Verna! It's great to see you!"

She smiled, returned his hug and said, "Bill, you're looking well for a father of three. Still hoping for a boy?"

"No, sadly, I think we're going to be content with the girls. Mary says there won't be a number four and you know what Mary wants is what Mary gets."

"How is Mary? Doing well, I hope."

"Yes, she's still the prom queen and my other commander. And what about you? Haven't met Mr. Right-Patterson yet?"

"That's a horrible pun, Bill, and just so you know, I've had a prospect or two and while it's hard to do, I think a girl can have a career and a husband."

"Well, what about that guy you went to high school with? What about him?"

"Oh, he's still around but I'm not ready to get serious just yet and he's pursuing his own career at the moment.

"Do you think he'll wait?"

"Verna smiled and replied, "If he knows what's good for him, he will."

"So, you're going to be one of my pilots. Who would have thought it? Small world, huh?"

"Seems so," she responded. "I'm looking forward to taking Pandora out of the Shepard Yard for her first flight next month."

"Well, Commander Jackson will have the final say about that, but who knows, it could be you. I've recommended you for Pandora's pilot but even if it's not you, co-pilot is good too… don't you think?"

"Thanks, Bill. Knowing you suggested me for pilot is endorsement enough for me, but if it's all the same, I'll be happy with pilot."

Collins paused a moment and then said, "Verna, I think you'll like Commander Jackson, once you get to know him, but be aware, he's old school. Well, what I mean is…"

"I know what you mean; he likes an all male ship. That's fine Bill; no need to worry. I've dealt with the type before. Thanks for the warning though."

The words had no sooner left her mouth when Collins saw Jackson go into his office. "Looks like the old man is here, so let's get the ball rolling."

Collins led her to the commander's temporary office and knocked on the door. "Enter," was the response from inside.

Collins opened the door and announced, "Sir, Captain Verna L. Starr, to see you."

"Good. Send her in and get some chairs. I want you to sit in on this."

"Yes, sir!"

Verna walked over to the commander's desk where they exchanged salutes. "Captain Starr, reporting for duty, sir."

"At ease, Captain. I'm Commander Jackson. I've asked you here at this time as a new member of my crew to go over a few things with you for clarification, just to make sure we're all on the same page. I have a few questions for you and I'm sure you'll have one or two of your own by the time we're finished." Collins had returned with two chairs and the commander began.

"Captain, let me start by saying I don't like to waste time. I prefer things to be open and direct and I don't like to coddle or sugar coat anything. How does that suit you?"

"Right down to the ground, sir."

"That's good, because I have to be honest and say that I have several reservations about you being a part of this crew. There are some things I can't quite get my mind around from your perspective and we're going to cover it all now. As I understand it, until recently, you were on your way to becoming the first U.S. woman astronaut and a pilot in SDF, but after your LM training at Shepard and saving yourself and the President's nephew from disaster, you were offered a pilot position aboard the Pandora, is that right?"

"Yes sir, that's correct."

"And you do know that officially, DSSF doesn't exist, don't you?"

"Yes sir, I understand DSSF does not officially exist."

"And you're still willing to give up all that would go with being the first female U.S. astronaut, the fame, the money, the advancement, endorsements and being a role model for other women?"

"Yes, sir, I fully understand what it means."

"You are aware that while you'll be the first U.S. woman in space, you can never tell anyone. No one can know, ever?"

"I understand, sir."

"The Pandora and her crew do not officially exist. Can you carry that secret to your grave?"

"Yes sir, I can."

"There is no official mission to Mars. There is no such service as DSSF."

"Let me assure you, sir, that I have no problem staying with my official dossier for life."

"Ok then, let's move on to the next item. Starr, your exploits as a fighter pilot are well documented and nothing short of amazing, so I'll give you a passing grade on that, but I still have a problem. I've been told that you possess extreme mental capabilities. Simply put, you make very smart look stupid. So, I just have to wonder, if you are such a genius, with the potential to make millions of dollars and pretty much do anything you wanted, why aren't you a doctor or an advanced research scientist, instead of risking your life in the military and space?"

"Well sir, it's never been about money or fame with me. Being a pilot and going into space has always been a dream of mine and it's the best way for a true scientist to understand the universe."

"Commander Jackson looked at her briefly then said, "It's also hard for me to believe your parents are comfortable with their little girl being a fighter pilot. I know I wouldn't want my only child going into combat, much less space."

Verna looked at Jackson seriously and replied, "I doubt any parent is ever comfortable with their child being in the military, male or female, but when I discussed my career choice with my parents my father only had two things to say about it. He said, 'Use your God given talents to understand His Kingdom, and… don't let your brains go to your head.'"

Commander Jackson laughed a moment and said, "I think I'd like your dad."

"I'm sure you would, sir. Everyone does."

"So you're saying your parents are just fine with you being an astronaut."

"Yes, sir."

"And do you have a spouse or significant other and are they ok with it all too?"

"I do, and he is behind me all the way."

Jackson groaned a little then said, "Here's another thing that bothers me, Captain, and this is why I wanted Collins to sit in on this, so I would have a witness to what I'm about to say. What are you, Captain, about 26, five feet three inches, 115 pounds? You've got waist length hair and you have quite a few more curves than any other crew member I've seen. In other words Captain, you are very attractive and you will be the only female in a crew of 33, and depending on how the mission goes, we might not be back home for over a year, maybe two. You don't see a potential problem with being the only female on board?"

"No sir, I don't."

"And, why not?"

Instantly, she very calmly, directly, and without batting an eye responded, "Because I trust you, sir, to maintain order and control of the crew."

Not expecting such a rapid and pointed response, Lt. Commander Collins was shocked when he heard her statement and he started to grin just a bit as the Commander shifted in his chair. She had caught him a little off guard, too, and he seemed flustered for just a moment but finally got out a sarcastic, "I'm glad to know you have such confidence in me, Captain."

Moving on with his diatribe Jackson continued… "And here's another little problem. Since you're new to DSSF and the only female, they haven't even developed a dress uniform for female enlisted, much less officers. Are you going to wear your flight suit all the time? We have to come up with some kind of officer's dress uniform for tomorrow's assembly. Or can you cobble up something tonight, Captain? I don't suppose you're a seamstress, too, are you?"

"Well, actually sir, I am. Sewing is a hobby of mine."

"Why am I not surprised?" Jackson lamented. "Is there anything you can't do?"

"Well, not many things, sir."

Jackson stood up and railed, "I wasn't looking for an answer, Captain, but I tell you what. You play Betsy Ross between now and tomorrow and see if you can come up with something appropriate for the crew assembly."

"Yes, sir. I'm sure I can alter one of my other dress uniforms. Would that be allowable, sir?"

Nearing his limit he almost yelled, "Fine! Just do it!" Then Jackson caught himself, took a deep breath and calmly stated, "Now, if it's not too much trouble, could we finish? Finally and frankly Captain, let me say that I disagree with many of my superiors in that I just don't think a woman's place is in space, especially DSSF."

"So what are you saying, sir? Do you intend to have me removed from the crew?"

"No, Captain, I have to follow orders too, so I have no such plans… for now. Actually, I already tried to have you removed and was told by my superiors how fortunate I am to have you as part of the crew. But know this, I will be watching every move you make and if I see anything less than perfection from you, you'll be confined to a Vindicator alone all the way home. Are we clear on that?"

"Yes, sir! Crystal clear!"

"Now, do you have any questions for me, Captain?"

"Yes, sir, I have two. Will the rest of the crew be held to the same standard of perfection that you have set for me?"

Jackson smiled just a bit then confirmed, "Of course, Captain, we are all held to the same standards.

She smiled back at him and said, "Then, sir, we should be just fine."

"And your other question?"

"Have you made a final decision on who will be the primary pilot for Pandora?"

Jackson answered, "The XO has suggested a name but I won't make my decision on that until the final roster is posted tomorrow at 1300. Now if you will excuse me, Captain, I have a lot of work to do before first assembly. Dismissed!" And with that, she and Collins stood, saluted, and left.

Once they were down the hall and outside of the building Collins looked at her and said, "Now that wasn't so bad, was it?"

Verna gave him a look of disbelief before she exploded, "Well, I suppose if you consider the Salem Witch Trials 'not so bad' then it was just peachy!"

"Oh, come on. He just wants to make sure he has the best crew. Give him a chance. He's a good commander."

"You keep telling me that, Bill, like I have a choice. Do I?"

"No, not really."

"That's what I thought. I just hope I get a fair chance to prove myself."

"Oh, you will. Trust me. You'll get your chance.

Arriving at his car, Collins offered to give her a tour of the cape and she agreed to go, provided there was a good place to eat along the way. "I need some food and a huge cup of Kona before we ride the day away." Then she looked at Collins almost in a panic and said, "Bill, there *will* be Kona on the Pandora, right? We can't go to Mars without Kona."

He looked at her and said, "The only way Kona will be on the Pandora is if you bring your own. The stuff they call coffee wouldn't pass for swill. I think they're still pushing that 'orange garbage' for the main beverage."

"Oh no! That orange poison won't do. That won't do, at all. Not for me!"

Collins laughed hard then pointed out, "You do know that we will be recycling *everything* on the ship, right? Do you understand what I mean by *everything?*"

"Yes, I do, but please, don't remind me. I prefer not to think about that. We had to recycle when I was going through Vindicator training at Shepard Yard and while those filters are very good and I honestly couldn't tell the difference between fresh and recycled, just the thought is enough to put me off of it." Collins laughed again and nodded his head in agreement.

The afternoon flew by as they visited every square inch of the installation. Toward the end Verna asked Collins straight out why they were really going to Mars, but he deflected her question and tried to change the subject. When she pressed him for an answer all he would say is that the crew would know soon enough but in the mean time all normal protocols applied. Normal protocol for DSSF was that DSSF does not exist, there is no Pandora, no secret base, nothing. All DSSF members had an alternate AFSC or MOS. Some even had alternate identities and that was one aspect of this branch of service she did not like at all, but the government had decided that what the average citizen didn't know wouldn't hurt them, and she had to go along with it.

After awhile Verna quietly complained, "You know Bill, when you're part of a covert branch of the military it causes you to be suspicious of everyone and everything."

"I understand how you feel Verna, and there will be times things won't look quite right to you, but that's when you have to trust protocol and that your fellow officers are doing the right things."

She said, "I understand that, I do. But trust isn't built in a day or a week and you are the only one I know here. I don't know anyone else in the crew. All I can do is follow orders and keep my eyes open."

"That's true enough. That is all you can do, but you've done well to this point. I see no reason to think that will change. Just trust your intuition."

"You can count on that," she replied.

As they arrived back at crew quarters she thanked him for the tour and for his advice. Collins said, "We better call it a day. Don't forget you still have to come up with something to use for a dress uniform."

"Oh, don't worry about that. I know what I'm going to do. Tell Mary I said hello and hug the kids for me."

"I will," he said. "You need to get a good night's sleep. Tomorrow will be a long day. PT and breakfast are at your discretion but meetings begin at 0700 and to accommodate you, first assembly with dress uniforms will be at 1300."

"Acknowledged. Meeting's at 0700, sir!"

"I guess this is good night, Captain."

"Good night, Bill." Verna closed her door and quickly went to work on her new uniform.

Thinking of how best to design a uniform that conformed to her coming assignment, she wanted her creation's appearance to be consistent with the other services. Her first thought for color came from the black and white roll pattern of the Saturn V vehicles and it would have been easy enough for her to do just that since she could just use her favorite black leather civi's, i.e. a biker jacket and mini skirt, matched with a white turtle neck and no sewing at all, but then she figured with all the resistance to females at the time, perhaps DSSF wasn't quite ready to be that modern. So after a little more thought, she opted for the standard Air Force dress whites. Having only a short time to work and limited resources, she had decided to convert a couple of her current Air Force togs into her vision of proper attire for a modern DSSF officer. With a snip here and a dart there she soon came up with her own original designs for a dress uniform and matching flight suit. Both were 100% polyester, form fitting and mostly white, with a bit of silver at key accent points.

The flight jacket was long sleeved with a full zip front, mainly white with silver accents across the shoulders with a slightly padded space suit style collar. The pants were completely white except for the outer thigh areas that were silver. The dress was also mostly white, long sleeved, with a full zip front. A three inch wide silver band ran down both sides, sleeves, and around the hem that was a full six inches above her knees. Everything was topped off with a slightly larger padded collar. In the end it was shorter than she had intended but she had used every scrap of material she had on hand and it just would have to do. Besides, she had the legs for it. To finish it all off she would also wear her favorite pair of black leather knee high boots.

Now well past midnight and finally having satisfied herself with the look and fit of each garment, Verna drifted off to sleep on the sofa. She needed all the rest she could get now, because in just a few hours the crew of the Pandora would assemble for the first time and begin work toward becoming a well oiled machine; the machine that would end alien abductions of humans forever.

Chapter 5

Verna had never owned an alarm clock but at precisely 0500 she suddenly woke from a sound sleep as if a switch had been flipped. In less than 60 seconds she was dressed and out the door for her morning PT. Running at a pace that would shatter her personal record for a 5 mile run she began to think about what the coming day would bring. For most of the world it would be just another December day, the usual grind, the same old routine, but the Pandora crew and a select few in high places knew differently.

The sun was breaking the horizon as Verna made it back to her room. Pleased to have shaved 24 seconds off her record she decided to reward herself with a large cup of Kona. It only took a few minutes to shower and put her hair up, and since dressing for the morning meetings would only require a standard flight suit, she was dressed and at her first meeting, cup in hand, with 10 minutes to spare.

Being the first to arrive afforded her the luxury of first choice for a seat. Looking the room over carefully she decided to keep a low profile and chose a chair in a rear corner that would allow her to see everyone else, but was only visible to the people on the platform. She had barely sat down when her crewmates began filing in and it was soon obvious that several of the men had been on previous missions together. Many seemed to be scanning the room for familiar faces and finding them. One or two had glanced in her direction but didn't take much notice at the time. Soon the room was buzzing as 30 men talked and waited for things to get started. While small groups of the crew had worked together on various missions in the past, they had never worked together as a whole. Forming them into one cohesive unit would be the first order of business for Jackson and Collins.

Instantly the moderate rumble of a room full of people ceased as XO Collins came in and barked, "Attention!" At that point everyone stood ram rod straight with eyes forward as Commander Jackson entered the room. He took the platform and stood silently behind the podium as he carefully looked over his new crew, studying their faces as though they were in a police lineup. A few he recognized; most he did not. He looked at each one's face until it had been burned into his memory but he stopped the longest when he got to Verna. His stare was so intense she could feel it. He was not pleased to have a woman among the crew but for now dealing with that would have to wait. He had more important issues at hand and they were about to get started. After a few tense seconds he finally spoke.

"Good morning! I'm Commander Jackson. I believe all of you have met our XO, Lt. Commander Collins. He will be assigning quarters, equipment, forming attack groups, scheduling practice missions and generally over seeing every aspect of your final preparations to fight in space. We have an historical mission off of this planet, and over the next 14 days this crew will become the most deadly fighting force in the history of mankind. All of you have been selected to serve aboard Pandora because you are already the most qualified personnel in your respective positions. You will listen to every word, instruction, and command, and perform every task and exceed every requirement placed upon you. From this moment forward, the people you see around you now are the only family you have, and you will give your life for any and every one of them, if needed. They are henceforward your brothers.

"I will not tolerate any form of disrespect, dissention or disharmony from anyone, or toward any member of this crew. In keeping with your oath you will not question or second guess any order, the ability of a crewmate, or me, *ever*! Again, those you see around you are now your only family. You will show the utmost respect and trust for your family. You will go above and beyond, *for your family*! Is that clear?"

The response to Jackson's query was an instantaneous and deafening, "SIR! YES, SIR! We are united. We are focused. We are one mind. We are one machine on a singular mission! We will be successful! Failure is not an option!" Again the crew loudly responded in one strong voice, "*Success or death!*"

Jackson paused a few seconds as he allowed the echo to fade to silence before he finished. Then almost in a whisper he repeated, "Success or death… let that sink in." The crew remained at full attention as Commander Jackson stepped off the platform and exited the room.

When Jackson had gone, Collins took center stage and began by saying, "From this point forward, and until preparations for the mission are completed, you will think of nothing else except your job and this mission! Beginning right now, there will be no form of outside contact permitted. You will however, be allowed to make a monitored phone call to your family to say good bye just prior to launch. For the next 14 days we require that all of your mental, physical, and spiritual energy be focused on your training. Just as an FYI, there will be a group of 31 men that will practice along side this crew, in case any of you wash out.

Now, as I call your name, step forward to receive your mission assignment and weapons. As soon as you have them go directly to the firing range for target practice and qualifications. We are not going to take a lot of time for this. You will be given 10 rounds for practice and 10 rounds for the test. You will use the weapons provided. Personal weapons are not allowed for this exercise. Anyone that doesn't qualify will be replaced. Is that clear?"

"Sir, yes sir!"

"You have 10 minutes to empty your bladders, hydrate, and/or pray before qualifications commence. Now, move it!"

The crew quickly moved to the firing range, with Collins and Verna bringing up the rear. As they walked along she asked him if he knew how many of the men had actual combat experience or had been in space. To her surprise he said, "All of them have seen combat at some point but only Bridge personnel have been in space at least once."

"Really? All of them have seen combat? Most of them don't look old enough to have served in Viet Nam."

Collins smiled, then explained, "Well, it's about a 60/40 split, as far as those who saw action in Nam. The rest have served in some capacity as 'advisors' in several different theaters over the last few years, and many of them have been in some horrendous battles no one has ever heard about. A few are Special Forces or former CIA operatives, but don't let their youthful appearance cause you to under estimate any of them. They are all very good at what they do and they all have more combat experience than you, much of it hand to hand."

Verna grinned and asked, "When have you ever seen me under estimate anyone, Bill?"

Collins glanced at her and cautioned, "To this point, never, but make sure you don't take anything or anyone on this mission for granted. Some of these guys walk very close to the line when it comes to ethics and morals. They are here because they have demonstrated the ability to perform a flawless mission and eradicate an enemy with extreme prejudice."

With concern, Verna stopped walking and asked Collins to look her in the eyes. Once she had his full attention she asked him if he doubted her ability to perform on the coming mission. Collins turned to her slowly, shaking his head and starting to smile, then paused. Looking very serious he finally said, "I'm only going to say this once, so listen closely, Captain. I have never had any doubts about *you*, at all, not ever, not from the first day I met you, until this instant. You are as pure and constant as sunshine, but there are things about this mission that cause me to question your safety."

"Why is that, Bill?"

"Two things," he replied. "Mostly, it's the mission, but also I'm a little concerned by the reputations of a couple of the crew and the way they may view you."

"Do you mean Commander Jackson?"

"No, not at all. Commander Jackson may not be overjoyed by your presence but he will always deal straight with you. He is honest and a "to your face" kind of man. What I mean is there are a couple of these guys that like to play by their own rules and have little respect for anyone, especially women. Just watch your back, ok? We'll talk more later, but for now let's catch up."

As they again walked toward the firing range they could hear the first practice shots being fired. The group had formed five separate lines and she fell into the closest line behind Collins. As they waited to receive their headphones and weapons she asked him what they would be doing next. Collins explained that everyone had to make a minimum score of 8 out of 10 on the primary 100 yard targets to continue the training, then those with the top three scores would compete for the number one position. "Sounds like fun to me," she said. "Good luck."

Collins turned to her and with a pleading voice said, "Just don't embarrass me when it's your turn, ok?"

The qualifications were proceeding at a good pace, and soon Collins was stepping up to the line with an M16. As he prepared to take his practice rounds the range safety officer loudly proclaimed, "XO on the firing line. Duck and cover!" A few of the men chuckled but then the line fell silent as all the others gathered around to watch.

Looking disgusted, Collins turned to the RSO and said, "Very funny, Jim. Thanks a lot. Maybe you should work in Vegas when you retire."

"Come on sir, let's see what you've got," came one voice from the far line.

"Aw, he can't even see the target. Somebody move it up for him. We won't tell."

Verna waited until they had finished their comments then quietly said, "Put a couple dead center Bill, and shut 'em up."

As he began his practice shots Collins pretended not to see the target and aimed close by, below or on either side, knocking up sand with each shot. "That's 10 misses out of 10 practice rounds," came the report from the field.

A few of the men began to chuckle and one even scoffed, "Maybe he really can't see the target."

Collins turned to the crowd and said, "That's pretty funny. Ha! Ha!" Then he winked at Verna, spun around and began firing. Ten rapid fire shots rang out, ten shots in under 5 seconds, and as he squeezed off the last one he quickly handed the rifle to the RSO, hot barrel first. He took the rifle but almost dropped it as he quickly moved his hand to the stock to keep from burning it. Collins score was 10 out of 10 rounds, inside the bull's eye!

Verna smiled and shouted, "Well, I guess he can see it after all!"

Once the RSO had secured Collins' weapon he called out, "Next up, Captain Starr," but as he started to say something cute about her she looked him right in the eyes. Her icy stare seemed to distract him for a moment, and all he said was, "Captain Starr on deck; practice rounds!" Verna turned to face the target and shouldered her M16. Without hesitation she also squeezed the trigger 10 times as fast as she could and waited for the report.

In a few moments she heard, "Starr, 10 for 10, in the bull's eye."

The RSO looked a little surprised then mumbled, "Nice work, Captain. Now let's see if you can do it again when it counts."

Without batting an eye Verna almost giggled, "No problem, but let's take it up a notch and use the target at 200 yards, shall we?" He smiled, then nodded his head in approval and stepped back. Verna glanced at Collins and winked then turned to face the secondary target and just as quickly clicked off 10 shots.

Again the man calling out the scores said, "10 out of 10, in the bull's eye, tighter grouping!"

The report was followed by a series of whoops and wolf whistles as she stepped down from the firing platform. Collins looked at her and cheered, "Yeah! That's what I'm talking about! Nicely done, Captain!"

"Thank you, sir. Should we stick around and watch the rest to see who our competition is going to be?"

"Fine by me," Collins said, and for the next half hour that's what they did. Soon everyone had successfully completed their qualifications and there were no surprises. The entire group had been cleared to move forward with mission training, and with qualification behind them they could now take a moment to compete for the top marksman position in the crew.

The RSO stepped back onto the platform and began again, "Listen up ladies. We now have the top 3 scores. Please step forward as I call out your names: Lutz, Collins, Starr. These three officers will now compete for Pandora DM using a standard issue DSSF 9mm pistol and the rifle of their choice. First up will be Lt. Lutz, followed by XO Collins and Captain Starr. The goal is to eliminate all close in minor targets in the field and the main long range target beyond the field. They will have 5 minutes to move through the course successfully. Each contestant has an electronic receiver that will signal if they are hit by the enemy. The one to eliminate all targets the fastest and without being eliminated themselves will be declared the winner. The competition begins in 15 minutes and for this round you may use a personal weapon or the rifle of your choice."

Verna turned to Collins and exclaimed, "Fifteen minutes! That doesn't give me very long." Then she jumped off the platform and jogged back to her room to retrieve her own rifle and returned just as the RSO was stepping up to the field microphone.

He began by saying, "Lt. Lutz will take the field first while Collins and Starr will be held in a sealed room so that they cannot see the course. When the bell rings the clock will start and they will have 5 minutes to eliminate all targets. Lt. Lutz, stand by and good luck to all."

Lutz stepped onto the field and motioned that he was ready. The bell rang and in less than five seconds he was under fire. He broke for the nearest cover but just before he got to it, a life size plywood image of a man holding a rifle popped up. On a dead run toward the image, Lutz quickly drew his 9mm and put two rounds through the image's head, knocking it over as he dove behind a simulated rock. Once there, he was quickly pinned down by heavy fire that seemed to be coming from all over. Lutz began firing back and as he did he was able to pick off two of the images. After knocking off two more he was able to continue down the course toward the last one that was firing at him.

The remaining image was really dug in but he had to get it before he could move on to the main target and he was running out of time. Looking over the terrain he decided the only way to take out the last image was to attack it from the rear. Knowing his time was growing short and after working almost two minutes to get in behind it, he was finally in position. Then just as he was about to take it out, four more images popped up. He managed to get two of them before they got him several times, causing his alarm to go off. After a few seconds a voice from down the range announced that, "Lt. Lutz is dead. Funeral arrangements to be announced. Send in the next victim!" Lutz muttered a few choice words under his breath as he cleared the range and Collins stepped up.

"XO Collins, standby!" The bell rang and the attack began as before with Collins getting the first image with one shot, but he didn't seek protection behind the rock as Lutz had. Collins chose to continue up the course on the left side. This time when the other images appeared, he was almost on top of two of them as they came up, but they were gone with just a couple of clicks. From this position Collins could easily see the remaining images and he used his personal M1 to drill them from relative safety. He was already way ahead of Lutz and hadn't even broken a sweat.

Only one remained in the dug in position and Collins cautiously moved toward it. Being a little more experienced, he was not so quick to charge in with guns blazing like Lt. Lutz. Instead he flanked the last one and tried to pick it off from a distance, but after a few near misses and the clock ticking, Collins began working his way toward the target again but not from the rear. He worked his way in from the side and was headed for a higher position. Once he got there it only took a single shot to take out the image, but in doing so he triggered the other four behind it and they kept him pinned down until his time had expired.

Verna stepped onto the platform just as Collins returned and took a seat next to Lutz. She looked at the RSO and asked if they were dead or just delayed. His reply was that Lutz was dead. Collins did well, but not well enough. She took a deep breath, looked at the field and said, "Let's do this!"

"Captain Starr, standby!" For the last time the bell rang and Verna began running up the right side of the field and was past the first image before it popped up. She spun around and nailed it twice before the other images opened up on her, and with them firing away she continued running up the right side of the course to the first cover she could find. This position put her above all of those shooting at her, including the dug in position. She caught her breath as she observed the field, carefully noting the source of fire in her direction. Then she began looking for the main target and after about a minute she found him almost a half mile away, apparently pacing next to some kind of vehicle.

Now that she was fully aware of her tactical position she would be able to go on the offensive. Setting up her rifle, she spread the legs of its tripod as she lay flat on the ground. Two quick taps right, another two left, one down on the dug in position and just that quick, her initial opposition had been eliminated, leaving her plenty of time to take out the main target, or so she thought. Just as she was turning her attention in that direction her forehead was hit by rock fragments from a ricochet. Then as she heard the sound of rapid shots being fired in her direction she could feel something warm running down her face. Instinctively Verna rolled on the ground with her rifle until she was behind a large oak tree.

Still hearing gun fire and live rounds hitting all around her Verna tried to wipe her face with her hand but it came back covered with blood. She looked at it a moment before wiping it on her jumpsuit and grabbing her rifle. Peeking out from behind the tree she couldn't see anyone on the range now. Everyone had taken cover. Then across the field about 200 yards away she saw a man running and firing at her as he went. He must be the one that had shot at her and he was moving fast but not quite fast enough. Even with the blood in her eyes blurring her vision and her blood pressure dropping fast, it only took a second to put the rifle to her shoulder, another to lock on target and less than another to tap the trigger twice. Between taps the man was only able to take one full stride, as the first bullet pierced the side of his skull and exited the opposite side through a much larger opening. The second round perforated his throat and the assassin hit the ground with a thud as his blood gushed everywhere. Verna then looked back at what was supposed to be the main target only to see the man and the vehicle were both gone.

As she staggered back down toward the firing line she could see Collins and Lutz running in her direction. Collins got to her first and said for her to lie down until help arrived but she assured him she was fine. "It's just a little scratch not much blood."

"Looks like you've lost a gallon to me," he said. "Now lay down until we get you checked out. That's an order!"

Verna managed a weak, "Yes, sir," and did as she was told.

She woke up about an hour later at the base hospital with 8 stitches along her hair line, wearing a flimsy hospital gown and surrounded by the E.R. doctor and several large men. As she became fully awake she reached for her blanket as she realized the entire crew was standing quietly in her room just staring at her. When she saw Commander Jackson standing there as well she tried to sit up and salute but her I.V. stopped her from fully raising her right arm. Jackson told her not to worry about all that for now, "…and by the way… nice shot! Where did you learn to shoot like that that? I saw the entire event from start to finish and you were amazing!"

"I was on the women's rifle team at Alabama. They do a lot more than just play football there, sir."

"Obviously," Jackson conceded with a chuckle.

Finally able to sit upright in her bed, Verna began looking around the room as though she had lost something. The doctor noticed and asked her what she was trying to find. She answered him by asking, "Where's Louise?"

"Louise?" the doctor asked. "Who's Louise? Was there another woman brought in?"

Collins answered him and said, "No, Doc. Captain Starr is the only female we've got."

"That's strange," he said, "I didn't see any signs of a concussion. Perhaps I should get another x-ray."

"At that point Marine Captain Johns spoke up and told them, "No need for an x-ray, doc. She's fine. She calls her rifle Louise. It's not unusual for Marine snipers to give their weapon a name.'"

After a moment, Lutz chimed in a bit puzzled with, "I thought she was Air Force, sir."

"I am, or I was, before DSSF. My rifle team coach at Bama was a Marine sniper. He taught me how to shoot and named my rifle Louise, for my alter ego."

"That figures," Johns said. "No Air Force brat I ever saw could shoot like that."

Verna looked right at him and said, "Watch it, Jarhead!"

"You watch it, Fighter Jock," he shot back, and the entire room erupted in laughter.

Collins looked at Jackson and whispered, "Sounds like we're becoming a family already." Jackson just nodded in agreement.

Commander Jackson asked if she could be released and the doctor said, "Yes, but she needs to get some rest today and drink plenty of fluids. I've given her 2 pints of blood, but she needs to build volume. She can return to training tomorrow, provided she takes it easy and whatever she does doesn't strain her stitches."

"No problem doc. She's a pilot. She won't be going hand to hand anytime soon. How's that suit you, Captain?"

"Right down to the ground, sir!"

Jackson just smiled. Then turning to Collins he told him to set things up for the following day, and then give the crew the rest of the day off.

As he left the room the doctor told everyone they needed to give her a little space so she could dress, and as they filed by her bedside they all gave her a high five. A few of the Marines made comments like "nice shot," "awesome shot," and of course Johns had to say, "Cute little nightie!"

Verna smiled and said, "I'll 'nightie' you, Jarhead!" Johns stopped by her bedside, locked eyes with her and said, "Ooo Rah, Air Force! Congrats on making DM."

"Ooo Rah! to you, too, sir. I'm glad you and your Marines will be going on the mission."

"Don't you worry about that, ma'am. We wouldn't miss this one for the world. We'll have your back. You just get us in position to do our job."

"Count on it, Jarhead. You'll be there."

When the last of the crew was gone Verna looked at Collins and Jackson and asked if they had identified the man she had shot. "Not yet, but we're still working on it, and that brings us to our first question. Do you have any idea why someone would want you dead?"

"No, sir; not a clue."

"You don't have any enemies?"

"No, sir; not that would want me dead. At least I don't think so. Perhaps someone else doesn't want me on your crew."

Collins thought a minute then suggested, "Or perhaps someone doesn't want you on this mission. That would make more sense to me."

"But why, sir? Just because I'm a woman?"

"No. Because you're very good at what you do."

"That would mean someone doesn't want this mission to succeed, sir."

"Perhaps. Could be someone you beat out for a position on the Pandora. I don't know, but for now you get some rest. We'll investigate it further. You just get ready to resume training in the morning."

"Yes, sir! I'll be there."

Just before Commander Jackson was about to leave she asked him how First Assembly had gone. "It didn't go, Captain. You couldn't be there, so we'll have that first thing in the morning before we resume training. You are a part of this crew now, and in time you'll see that we work together, we play together, we live together and if necessary, we die together, but whatever we do, we do it together."

"I understand sir. It's nice to have family, sir. So, you haven't posted the pilot position for Pandora yet?"

"No, Captain, not yet."

His answer caused her to smile a little and that stretched a few of her stitches, changing her expression from one of happiness to a child like pout.

"All positions will be announced in the morning, Captain. Oh, and by the way, how is it going with a dress uniform for you? Were you able to come up with anything for First Assembly?"

"Yes, sir, I have two uniforms."

"Excellent! Well then, we'll all be looking forward to that. Now, I have a few things to take care of before morning, so if you and Mr.

Collins will excuse me, I will see you both at 0800."

After Jackson and Collins had stepped out of the room, Starr dressed while Collins waited to take her back to her quarters. It was a short trip from the hospital and in a few minutes he was walking her to her door, yet again. "Ok, Captain, here you are safe at home. In the morning you have First Assembly at 0800, then some major time in the simulator, and to that end I have a little surprise for you."

Verna frowned a bit then warned him, "Now, Bill, you know I don't like surprises. What's up?"

"Oh, I think you'll like this one. You're going to get to work with an old friend."

"Really? Who?"

"Major Knowles."

"Really! Mike's going to be here?"

"He's going to be more than here. He's now assigned to the Pandora."

"That's great! He was fantastic when I was at Houston. It will be good to have another friend onboard."

"Well, there you go; something to look forward to," Collins said. "Now, you get some rest and if all goes well you'll be working with Major Knowles in a Vindicator simulator again in the next day or two practicing takeoffs and landings."

"That's a wonderful surprise, Bill. Thank you! I can't wait!"

Chapter 6

Day two of final training would begin with the entire crew gathering at the base auditorium in full dress uniform for first assembly, and it was there that Commander Jackson would announce his assignments for command pilot, co-pilot, and commander, air group.

XO Collins had been at the auditorium since 0600 making sure everything was exactly as Commander Jackson required, and by 0730 Collins had it all ready to go, including live two way communications to the Pentagon. The only thing he had to be concerned with now was the new dress uniforms. While there were only one or two minor variations, the DSSF dress whites closely resembled those of the U.S. Navy and Collins thought that since this would be the first time many of the crew had worn theirs he would inspect them all before assembly to make sure they were dressed according to regulation. Stationing himself at the main door put him in a perfect position to inspect the crew as they arrived.

Thirty minutes later and just seconds before Commander Jackson arrived, Collins breathed a sigh of relief as the last man passed inspection, emphasis on last *man*. As he stepped onto the platform and took his last visual check of the crew he suddenly realized there was a vacant place right in the center of the front line and Verna was no where to be seen. Then just as he was about to panic, Collins saw Commander Jackson walk through the door with Captain Starr close behind, but when he saw her, he almost fell off the platform.

To this point the men had thought Starr was kind of cute in her slightly baggy flight suits, no makeup and hair up in a bun. Most of them considered her to be somewhat of a tomboy, but her design for the DSSF female dress whites left Collins and every other man there almost speechless. Her dress was white alright; very form fitting, and the hem only came to her finger tips, about six inches above her knees. From head to toe she was a series of very nice curves, especially her well toned legs, and she no longer looked like a tomboy. Contrasted by her black boots, long brown hair and topped with the traditional Navy women's dress cap, there was no way she would ever be taken for a "man in uniform."

Jackson turned and walked up the ramp to the podium while Verna only had to walk five or six steps to take her place, but in the time it took her to do so, she had the full attention of every man in the room. Collins called a garbled, "*Attention!*" for Commander Jackson, but the men were already at attention, for Starr. After a few seconds of watching the men trying to get a look at her, Collins quietly said, "Eyes forward!"

An overhead projector clicked on behind Jackson and Collins, and they could all see a podium with the Presidential Seal on the screen.

At that point Commander Jackson began, "At ease! After reviewing yesterday's results for weapons qualifications, I am pleased to announce that everyone has qualified to continue training. As for the incident on the range, we are still investigating every piece of evidence. There is no new information at this time as to who or why anyone would try to kill Captain Starr but I can tell you that preparations for launch are on schedule and will continue uninterrupted. Captain Starr has been cleared to continue… and I suggest that no one challenge her on the range."

His comment drew a loud "Ooo Rah!" from Captain Johns.

"Ooo rah, indeed," continued Jackson. "Her response to an unexpected lethal situation was the most amazing display of 'cool under fire' and marksmanship I have ever witnessed. You men should be proud to have Captain Starr as part of our crew. Because she qualified for the DSSF so quickly and given the fact that Captain Starr is the first woman to serve with us, there was not enough time for command to design a woman's dress uniform. I therefore commissioned Captain Starr to design her own uniform and she has done so with only the supplies she had on hand. I met with her this morning and approved her design until command can come up with something of its own.

"Now, over the next few days we will be practicing several scenarios with the various teams. For the last three days of training we will bring everyone together and execute our mission as one unit until you can do anything and everything in your sleep or complete darkness. Now, if you will direct your eyes to the screen, the President has a few words to say. Mr. President…" Jackson and Collins turned toward the screen and as they did the President stepped to the podium.

"Good morning, Pandora crew! At this time I want to convey to you how proud I am to be your Commander in Chief. The mission that lies ahead of you is one of paramount importance, and while all of the details of your mission cannot be revealed at this time, I am certain that when you are fully aware of its scope and magnitude, you will respond as all great Americans have since Valley Forge. While our primary concern is for our own country you will also be performing a tremendous service for all mankind. Let me assure you that nothing you will ever do will be as important as this mission.

"Your ship bears the name Pandora. The name was chosen for a reason that will become clear to you soon. You will be the first American space warship to cruise the solar system, but others will follow shortly. You won't be out there alone for long, but in the mean time you have sole responsibility for the security of our nation and our world. Those who remain here will be praying and depending on you to preserve our freedom and way of life. Good luck and God speed!"

The screen faded as Jackson stepped back to the microphone. "Thank you, Mr. President. It's now time to announce my selections for command pilot, co pilot and CAG. When I call your name, step to the front and face the crew. CAG, Major Michael Knowles. Command pilot, Major Bryan Connor. Co-pilot, Captain Verna Star."

When he had finished Jackson nodded to Collins, and once they were front and center Collins came down from the podium with three small boxes, each containing the appropriate insignia for their new assignments. In turn, he faced each one, placed the insignia on the uniform, and exchanged salutes. Per DSSF protocol, Collins attended to each of the majors before Captain Starr, but once he got to Verna, as he was attaching the frogs he leaned in and whispered, "I always save the best for last. I hope you're not too disappointed." She however, did not respond, keeping her eyes forward and face expressionless. Collins stepped back and saluted her, then returned to his place next to Commander Jackson.

After a brief pause to again look over the crew, Jackson resumed speaking. "Some of you may be wondering about DSSF and the make-up of this crew. Of necessity, Pandora's crew consists of personnel from all four branches of the military but that is not because DSSF wants to be democratic or inclusive. It is because no single branch of service can provide all the skills required at the next level: that of space based operations. It requires the best from of all of us! All future missions will employ every aspect of each branch. Each of you represents the absolute best of your respective branches and no less than your best will be acceptable. I know only a handful of you have ever been in space but I also know you will all adapt there, as easily as you have adjusted to the blending of ranks and protocols of DSSF. Lord knows, we certainly have our share of commanders, majors, and captains. Just keep in mind that as long as each one of us does his or her job, everything else will fall into place. Trust command, trust your team leaders, and trust yourselves. Gentlemen, our time is short and the task is great. Let us be about our business. XO Collins will now direct you to your next training exercise."

With that, Collins took the mike and began instructing the crew as to where they should go next. "Training will resume at 1300 hours. Each team report to your respective training facility: pilots report to your simulators; Rangers and Marines to the firing range; Pandora support personnel report to the mock-up building."

As Collins was about to send them on their way he noticed Sergeant Boyd looking at him with his hand up. "Do you have a question, Boyd?"

"Yes, sir."

"What is it?"

"Well sir, I'm kind of new to all of this and we don't have any women in the Rangers that look like Captain Starr, so I was just wondering if there are other women in DSSF that look like her, or is she the only one, because most of the military women I've seen look like Franklin's wife, you know, like a pug in uniform?"

Before Collins could answer Franklin quickly spoke up and stormed, "You near-sighted hillbilly! My wife might be on the plain side but at least she doesn't need a full set of theatre curtains just to make herself a pair of panties!"

Collins stood there stunned for just a moment as he tried to figure out what was happening but seeing that things were about to get out of hand he yelled, "ATTENTION!" The command had the desired effect as the entire crew stood still and quiet. "All of you will remain silent and report to training on the double! I don't want to hear another word! Not one word! Dismissed!" As they jogged away, Collins wondered to himself how some of these men would ever stand being in space for up to two years. It's going to be a long voyage!

Once Sergeant Brown and Captain Baker reached the firing range, Brown quietly said to him, "You know, sir, I don't know why he got upset. Franklin's wife does look like a pug."

Baker gave him a look of disbelief, then after a few seconds the two of them laughed and nodded in agreement. "I know, Sergeant, but how about we stay out of it. Just because something is true doesn't mean you have to say it."

"You're right, sir, but Collins didn't answer the question. Is Starr the only one?"

"I believe so." he concluded. "Even if there are other women, I'm pretty sure Starr is one of a kind."

"Oh," Brown said sadly. "I was hoping to find me a girl friend."

Baker laughed and promised, "If we make it back, I'll introduce you to my cousin, Sue."

"Is she pretty, sir?"

"Well, she ain't a pug, and she doesn't have to make her panties from old curtains."

Over the next several days, training proceeded at a rapid pace and without interruption as each team worked toward peak efficiency. There were no injuries, no mishaps, and all was going well. Daily, Jackson and Collins evaluated every team and made the needed adjustments to reach the overall objective.

Week one was a blur to most of the crew as the day began before dawn and ended in the wee hours of the morning. Long grueling hours of assaults and counter assaults were executed by the Marines and Ranger teams, while the pilots felt as though they had been imprisoned in their simulators. Support crews were stretched to their limits keeping up with all the supply demands of every team. Even the senior officers were showing signs of stress as they all worked to maintain their edge over eighteen hour days but somewhere along the way the crew got their second wind. Their scores and success ratings rose to near perfect, even after they had gone three days without food or sleep.

As day seven was ending, Collins noticed that Commander Jackson was smiling for the first time in at least a week. Walking over to him he said, "Well, there's a sight I never thought I would see again."

"What's that?" Jackson asked.

"You smiling, sir."

"Well, that's because they are finally getting it. They have their edge now; the blade is almost sharp enough. I'm satisfied with each individual team's performance under pressure. It's time to bring them all together for a dry run, but first we'll give them a full day of R&R. Go tell them."

Collins practically ran to inform the crew that they had a day off before coming together to complete training. The news of a much needed day of rest was met by several whoops and yelps of gratitude. "Get some rest gentlemen; you've earned it."

Verna eased up behind Collins so quietly that when he turned around to go he nearly knocked her down. "Hey! Watch it Captain! You're very sneaky aren't you?"

"I suppose I can be, sir."

"Who taught you to be so quiet? That Indian boyfriend of yours?"

"Maybe," she answered smiling brightly. "He's taught me a few other things over the years, too."

"I bet he has… So, tell me Captain, what are you going to do to relax on your day off? Sleep, run, read a tech manual? How about an encyclopedia?"

"Nah, I don't think so. I've already read plenty of those. If I had access to a plane I would go flying but then, being just a lowly captain, I don't know where I could get one, do you? After all, it's not like I have any friends here that could help me, do I?"

"Hey! I thought we were friends."

"Yeah, me too but that depends on whether or not you can get me a plane."

"What about your stitches? Can you wear a helmet?"

"Yes, yes, they're gone. Got them out this morning."

"Ok, then, I might be able to swing something small… for an hour or so. Call me after 0900 in the morning and I'll see what I can do."

"Oh, that would be great, Bill! You're the best friend ever! See you in the morning!"

"Wait. Don't be too excited. I don't have a plane, yet."

"Oh, you will. I have tremendous faith in you! See ya!"

After a great night's sleep Verna almost jumped out of bed and ran to the phone to dial up Collins. The ringing jolted him awake and he knocked the phone to the floor as he tried to answer it. Sleepily he said, "Hello! What? Who's there?"

"Hey, Bill, it's your best friend. Let's go flying!"

Still half asleep, Collins was trying to figure out who was calling him. "Verna? Captain? And I say Captain for the moment… what time is it?"

"I don't know, sir, a little after 0600, I think."

"0600! I told you after 0900!"

"Yes, well, it's been light out forever and the sky is perfect! Let's go! Where should I meet you… best friend?"

"I don't know. I have to shower and get dressed and get some chow. I don't know. Meet me at the main gate in an hour."

"That's great!"

Collins began muttering to himself like he was in an old Jimmy Stewart movie as he struggled to get out of bed. "0600 in the blessed morning! Best friend… maybe I don't want a best friend! I have a wife and kids. I don't want any more friends! The first day off in a month and my 'best friend' turns out to be a nuclear powered, gung ho, jet jockey… Wait, can a woman be a jet jockey? I don't know. Where are my pants? Can't find my shoes… I guess I need to shower first anyway, and where am I going to get a plane for her to go play with?"

Arriving at the main gate, Collins found Verna standing just inside the guard shack already wearing her flight suit, helmet in hand. "I'm glad to see you slept well, Captain. I was not so fortunate. Some nut called me at the crack of dawn to test my phone and my patience!"

"You should report that, sir. We can't have people playing pranks with official government property. So what did you reserve for us?"

"Oh, it's not much; just a small plane."

Changing her tone to one of disappointment she said, "Well, that's ok, sir. I didn't really expect much. I'm sure you did your best. It's just that I haven't flown in several weeks now, and if I have to spend any more time in the Vindicator simulator I think I'll scream! I'm getting claustrophobic! I need to fly something! Anything! Just get me in the air!"

"Ok! Ok! Calm down, Captain! We'll get you in the air shortly. Geez! I was only able to reserve a small plane but as you say, it is a plane and it will get you off the ground." Then as they rounded a large brick building, her eyes came to rest on a sparkling, almost new, F-15.

"Bill, is that the little plane you were talking about?"

"Yes, that's it. It's just a small one but it will get you off the ground."

"Oh, yes, it will. It certainly will! I knew my best friend wouldn't let me down."

Verna had the door open and was out of the car before it stopped rolling. "Hey, can I get parked before you fire it up and blaze into the blue?"

"You are stopped!"

"Well yes, I'm stopped now and you'll be interested to know that there's no ground crew for us," he said, as he went to retrieve his helmet from the trunk.

"No problem. I'll get the chocks. Did you file a flight plan?"

"Nope, didn't know we needed one. I thought you just wanted to play around for a bit."

"That's fine," she said as he began climbing into the front seat. "Hey! Where do you think you're going, Mister? If you're coming along, you're in the back!"

"Really? After I get you a plane, and not just any plane but one of our best jets, I have to ride in the back?"

"That's a roger, sir. You just sit back and enjoy the ride."

As Collins got settled into the back seat he could hear Verna going down the checklist and feverishly flipping switches to get her new toy spooled up and running. "Oh my! Listen to that! There's nothing quite like a pair of turbo fans spinning up to get your heart to pumping. It still gives me goose bumps."

"Verna, you are so funny sometimes. You sound like a teenage boy in love with his fast car."

"Exactly," she said. "It's raw power at my finger tips."

Soon the fastest and best fighter in the U.S. arsenal was purring and ready to go. "Bill, I can feel it! I can feel it in my right hand!"

"Feel what?"

"Fifty thousand pounds of thrust!"

"You know, Captain, you are beginning to scare me just a bit. Maybe this is a bad idea."

"Oh relax, sir. We're just going up for a little spin. No big deal."

"That's good to know. I guess it will be ok, then, when you're ready. Wait! What do you mean by spin, exactly?"

"All clear, sir?"

"All clear, Captain." And with that she eased them onto the taxi way. "It's good to hear the sweet familiar whine… of a turbine! Ohhh, just listen to that," Verna said as the canopy locked in place. "Let's see what she can do! I believe Mach 2.5 is reachable, don't you?"

"I was afraid you were going to say something like that. How about we keep in mind that I'm responsible for this one, so let's try to bring her back in one piece, ok?"

"Roger, sir. One piece!"

Then as she pulled away from the line she contacted the tower. "A.S. tower. Eagle 1 requesting permission for takeoff."

"Affirmative, Eagle 1. I have you. Proceed on current heading to main runway and hold."

As they reached the main runway they had to wait just a moment for a 747 to land. "We should be clear to go in just a minute, Bill. Are you strapped in tight?"

"As tight as I can be. How about let's not test the strength of the belts this time around, ok?"

"I won't, sir."

In about 30 seconds the tower was back on her headset. "Eagle 1, you are cleared for takeoff. Have a nice flight."

"Roger. Eagle 1 departing." Collins braced himself as he felt the afterburners kick in and push him deep into his seat, but Verna didn't do her usual roll to vertical takeoff. Instead, she rolled about halfway down the runway and leisurely lifted off.

The sky was crystal clear as they continued to climb to angels 10 with visibility more than 30 miles. "Wow, look at that Bill. You don't see this kind of visibility along the coast very often now, do you?"

"No, can't say you do; and the water is beautiful!"

"Where would you like to go this morning sir? The Bermuda Triangle, a low pass over the Keys? Maybe we could buzz the Homestead Tower?"

"Well, that all sounds like fun, Captain, but let's just keep it smooth and steady, ok? Oh, I know, let's make a low pass over Daytona Beach and wake up some people."

"No, no, let's don't and say we did."

"I don't think that's a good idea Captain."

"Sure it is. Here we go!"

In less than a second she was into a 180 and a steep dive.

"Whoa, Captain! Can we go back up and get my gut?"

"Oh, come on, you love it as much as I do. Stop complaining."

"I knew it! I knew the nice ride wouldn't last; crazy woman driver!"

"You mean crazy woman flyer don't you?"

"I guess that depends on how low you go over the beach now, doesn't it?"

Coming in from the south at 500 knots and 100 feet off the water, she lined up on Daytona and paralleled the beach. I tell you what sir, just to be on the safe side we'll stay about 100 yards off the water's edge. Will that make you happy?"

"No, but you're going to do it anyway."

"Yep, here we go sir!"

As she began her run, the beach was covered with Snow Birds, some walking ankle deep in the chilly surf. "Look at all those people enjoying themselves down there. You could almost reach out and touch them!"

"If you get any lower they may reach out and touch us!" The F-15 roared past just a stone's throw off the beach, deafening most of those along the way.

After she had gone a couple of miles, Verna decided it was time to climb. "Are you ready back there?"

"I'm almost afraid to ask 'ready for what' but I guess so. What are you…" But he didn't get to ask his question as they suddenly were vertical and angled back out over the water. They continued their climb for almost a minute, and then she leveled off at 25,000.

"Still with me sir?"

"I… I… think so, but if you do anything like that again someone is going to have some cleaning to do in this plane. We've been up almost an hour and it looks like about half of our fuel is gone. What do you say we head back? You know how Dad hates it when you bring the car home empty."

"Fine, we can head back. I do feel better now."

"That's good, Captain. Live to tell the tale. That's what I always say."

"Fair enough. We're only 30 miles out. I'll have us home in just a few minutes, sir, and you'll be safe and sound."

The time in the air was like a tranquilizer to Verna. She was as relaxed as she had been in quite some time, but just as she began a long turn back toward the base, her alarms went off. "What the heck!"

"We've got incoming, Captain!"

"What! From where?"

"Looks like we have company on our 6 about three miles back. I'm tracking one missile closing fast!"

"Hang on, sir. We're going evasive. I'm popping chaff and flares." Verna dumped about a dozen flares as she rolled and dove for the deck with Collins calling out time to impact. 5..4..3.. Verna gunned her engines and banked hard into the missile causing it to miss their plane by less than 20 feet before finally going into the ocean.

"Man, that was too close," Collins screamed, as he tried to relocate the aggressor.

"Roger, too close, sir. So, I guess now isn't a good time to point out that we're not armed. That's just marvelous, sir! Leave it to you to get us an unarmed plane."

"Hey, don't blame me. I didn't know we were going to play this game.

"So, we don't have rockets. What about guns?"

"Yes! We have guns… but no ammo."

"This just keeps getting better and better, sir. I always wanted to go into combat unarmed!"

Just at that moment they could hear the pinging of bullets hitting their plane like hail on a tin roof. Instantly she rolled down and away trying to escape the incoming fire while Collins quickly checked all the systems for damage.

"The starboard engine is on fire! Shut it down!"

Verna killed her starboard engine and pushed the remaining engine to full throttle as she tried to get some altitude. "Can you tell what he's flying, sir?"

"Yes, I think it's another F-15."

"Wonderful," she barked in a sarcastic tone.

Lead passed all around them as she twisted and rolled, up and down. Seemingly she was in full panic mode but there was method to her madness. "What the heck are you doing, Captain? He's all over us! Level off. Let's bail and take our chances!"

"Hang on, sir. I understand him now."

"What? You understand him?"

"Yes, sir, his pattern. I've got this."

"Well, I feel so much better now, Captain. I didn't know you were telepathic, too. That explains a lot. You should have told me sooner that you had it all well under control. I was beginning to worry." Verna ignored the sarcasm coming from the rear seat and snapped her wounded jet back to vertical, followed closely by the assassin.

"Everyone has a pattern of attack. All you have to do is learn their pattern and take advantage of it."

"Oh, is that all? And you picked this up in less than 30 seconds?"

"Yes, actually, I did. How many times did I defeat you, sir?"

"Ok, I get your point, but we're not armed. How is 'knowing his pattern' going to help us now?"

"Well, for one thing, he's trying to stay in our blind spot and he's overly aggressive for another. We can use that against him."

"I'll say he's overly aggressive. He's nearly up our exhaust! Do you think he knows we're unarmed?"

"Since he obviously knew we would be up here and where to find us, I'd say so. He probably checked out our plane before we arrived or he could even have been the person that got it to you sir."

Still twisting and banking hard, she said, "OK, Bill, this is it. He's right where I want him. We're going to do a complete loop and dive for the deck, and I mean we're going low. With only one engine I can't do this as fast as I would like. We have to be able to pull out, but I still think it will work. When we come around and go vertical again, as he begins his climb behind us, I'm going to deploy and release our chute. Hopefully the chute will open enough to cover his canopy rendering him blind or maybe even get sucked into his intakes. I need you to watch him and tell me when to release the chute. Two seconds later I'm also going to release our tail hook. Got it?"

"I think so."

"Ok, here… we… go!"

Arcing over, they screamed toward the deck with the intruder right on their tail, guns still blazing away.

"Call it, sir!"

"Get ready, Captain…3,000… 2,000… 1,000…"

"Roger. Pulling up now!" With the fuselage creaking from the maneuver and the remaining engine groaning as though it might explode, slowly they began to pull out of the dive. After a second or two they were level and then a second later she began to climb almost straight up. Right on cue the bogie was still following and beginning his climb right behind her.

"Get ready… now captain!"

"Chute away!"

"Wait, wait, now!"

"Hook away!"

As though it had been scripted, the chute did not fully deploy but it opened enough to completely cover the canopy of the trailing F-15 as its nose centered the chute. An instant later the tail hook cratered his left wing and ripped a large hole in the fuel tank. "We got him!" Collins screamed. "I don't believe it, but we got him!"

Verna quickly made a sharp turn toward the base and made a run for home. "Eagle 1 to A. S. Tower. I am declaring a May Day! We are under attack and badly damaged. I need to make an emergency landing."

"Roger, Eagle One. We are clearing the air space and rolling emergency crews now. We have you 18 miles out at 4,000 feet."

"Bill, what happened? Where did he go?"

"I don't know. Last thing I saw was him spiraling up and out to sea. I lost him when you bugged out, but he's not back there now. I don't know where he went."

"Eagle 1, did you say you were under attack?"

"That's affirmative. We were attacked by another F-15 but don't know who it was or where he went."

"Roger, Eagle 1. Scrambling interceptors now."

In seconds the entire installation went on alert and a pair of F-15's armed to the teeth rolled down the runway and lifted into the sky. In less than a minute Verna saw them passing directly over her, already supersonic and on their way to find a blind F15 with a damaged left wing.

"So much for our smooth little ride," Collins said. "You know, they're going to fry us when we land."

"I don't think so, sir. All we did was defend ourselves."

"Yes, but we have a severely damaged jet, and we're supposed to be relaxing. Somehow, I don't think Commander Jackson or anyone else will be pleased to see us, provided we walk away from the landing."

"Walk? We'll be riding away sir. Just sit tight. Are you ok?"

"I think so, but my wits may never be the same."

"Eagle 1 you are cleared for final approach on 13. Emergency crews standing by. Good luck!"

"Roger, A.S. tower. I have the lights. We're coming home. Ding! The captain has turned on the no smoking sign. Please close your tray and return your seat to its upright position."

"Bill, why don't you sing something while I get us on the ground?"

"Sing? About what?"

"I don't know. How many songs about a girl named Mary have there been, a million? I don't know… I don't know." After a few seconds she asked him, "Bill, why aren't you singing?" Collins didn't answer. "Bill? Are you still back there?"

"Yes, I was just thinking of all I could have lost today. There's more than Mary you know."

"Cheer up. You were never in real danger. You were with me. Still best friends?"

"I suppose."

"Good! On the numbers in 5..4..3..2..1.. touchdown! And thank you for flying, *Starr Airlines!* If you have enjoyed your flight please let the captain know and don't forget to tip the stewardess."

"And thank you, God!" Collins added.

Without a chute and only one reverse thruster, Verna eased the crippled bird down to taxi speed. "A. S. Tower, please thank the boys for turning out today, but I think we're ok now."

"Roger, Eagle 1. Please turn right at P 2. Ground crew will direct you from there."

"Roger, Tower. Eagle 1, out."

As they made their way to the hangar, Verna could see a large contingent headed in their direction. She taxied to within inches of the waiting ladder and raised the canopy. "Good afternoon, airman! If you would be so kind as to check the tires and clean the windshield, we would greatly appreciate it." He just looked at her funny and stood next to the ladder as they climbed down. Once on the ground they were greeted by Commander Jackson, Major Knowles and most of the crew.

Collins was the first one to reach planet Earth and as he did he went down on all fours to kiss the ground. He was there so long that Verna nearly stepped on him as she came off the ladder. Once he was sure he was safe again he stood up and they saluted Commander Jackson, who looked to be very upset and said, "Well, ladies and gentlemen, I can't wait to hear this one! Are you two alright?"

"Yes sir. Perfectly sir."

"Yes, thank God, we're fine."

"Good. How about we all go into my office and you tell us EXACTLY WHAT HAPPENED!" Jackson screamed.

Collins looked at Verna and said, "I told you he wasn't going to be happy."

The group moved into Jackson's office while Starr and Collins described their ordeal and how they got out of it. Except for the participants, the others were speechless as they sat spell bound listening to their story. Finally Jackson said, "I have to say that if I had heard this story from anyone else I'd say you were both liars, but given Starr's reputation, it will go down as another remarkable instance in her permanent records and of course, a nice assist by Lt. Commander Collins."

Just then an airman appeared at the door and handed the

Commander a message. Jackson paused a moment to read it then shared the report with the others.

"This is not good news. According to DSSF HQ, they have been unable to identify the man that attacked Starr on the gun range, and now it appears the interceptors not only brought down your attacker but the plane sank in deep water, taking the pilot with it. It may take weeks to recover the body and that's unfortunate because we still don't know who or why someone wants to kill Starr. We all need to remain on guard for anything or anyone acting suspicious. I think that about sums it all up. Everyone is dismissed except Collins and Starr."

As the last man left, Jackson turned to Collins and Starr and said, "All we know for sure about the first man is that he was hired to make a hit on Starr, but without capturing the pilot that came after her today, we probably won't learn anything new from that encounter either. We don't know yet where they got the F-15 or how they knew Starr would be flying today, or where, for that matter. Until we do, we are taking every precaution to secure the base and crew. All we know for sure is that he was not U.S. military."

"I don't understand, Commander. Why would two men be willing to die just to keep a woman off the Pandora?"

"It's more than that," Jackson continued. "I don't think it's about a woman on the Pandora so much as keeping her talents and abilities off the ship. What do you think, Captain?"

"Well sir, I don't think they intended to die. I think they simply under estimated their opponent. People have been doing that with me all my life, but as to why they want to kill me, I haven't a clue."

"We'll find out in the end," Jackson said, "but for now we need to stay focused and on schedule. All that matters at this time is coming together as one unit. Mr. Collins, is everything in order for the crew's first day of practice on the Pandora mock up?"

"Yes, sir. At 0600 tomorrow morning I have five exercises planned. Pending satisfactory scores, we'll practice a complete launch the following day. Once we have it all down pat, we'll practice as many times as possible leading up to launch day."

"Sounds good to me," Jackson said.

The next morning the crew worked through every exercise and all phases of the mission several times. As expected, the first run was a bit slow and stiff, but each successive run saw rapid improvement in their understanding and performance. By 1400 they were performing as though they had done it all hundreds of times and after a quick break for an MRE they were back, hard at it again. The men were coaching and encouraging each other as they went, intent on nothing less than perfection. By 1600 they had stored their checklists and were performing all functions at near peak efficiency. Collins had originally scheduled the day to end at 1900, but when he called them all together the crew wanted to run through everything one more time.

When he heard the crew wanted to have one more dry run before calling it a day, Jackson smiled for the second time in a month. "What do you think of that," Collins asked, grinning from ear to ear. "They've been at it all day and they still want one more run. They don't want to stop until it's all perfect."

"Dad gum right!" Jackson roared. "We've got us a good crew."

"Agreed," Collins answered. "One more for today, then we'll do it all again tomorrow."

"XO! Tell them one more time!"

"Aye, sir! Ok, you bunch of gold bricks. Let's do this one more time!"

Over the next three days they practiced relentlessly and by the time they were finished every one of them could indeed perform their jobs in their sleep. At the end of the last day and after the final dry run Jackson had the crew gather together in the cafeteria for a steak dinner and a short briefing.

When they had finished eating, Jackson stood up and began to speak. "Crew of the Pandora, I want to tell you all how pleased and proud I am with your efforts, enthusiasm, and commitment to perfection. As the President has said, no matter what else you do in this life, it will never be more important than this mission. This crew is ready! Our ship is ready! Mankind is ready! What say ye?"

Then standing to their feet, they all replied, "Success or death!" Jackson nodded in agreement and said, "Amen. Be seated. At this time Mr. Collins will read the names of all those who have successfully completed training and their assignments. Mr. Collins, if you will…"

Collins stood and began, "Ladies and gentlemen, the official roster of the U.S.S. Pandora:

Commander: Carl Jackson
Lt. Commander / XO: Bill Collins
Chief Medical Officer: Lt. Commander Ronald Patel
Commander Air Group: Major Michael Knowles
Command Pilot: Major Bryan Connors
Co Pilot: Captain Verna Starr
Computer Sciences / Chief Engineer: Major Blake Driskill
Communications Officer: Lt. Peter Ryan
Flight Engineer: Senior Master Sergeant Mark Fontaine
Vindicator Pilots:
    Major Emmett DeArman
    Major Charles Thomas
    Captain Kent Lutz
    Captain Richard Williams
    Captain John Shell
    Captain William Fuller
Marines:
    Captain Troy Johns
    1st Lt. Jack Casey
    Sergeant Ronald Tanner
    Specialist Cleveland Harris

    Specialist Henry Fisk
    Specialist Anthony Dietl
Rangers:
    Captain Robert Baker
    Sergeant Wyatt Brown
    Sergeant Walter Briggs
    Sergeant George Franklin
    Sergeant Edward Holcomb
    Sergeant Patrick Boyd
Enlisted:
    Airman 1st class James Miller
    Airman 1st class Stephen Swain
    Airman 1st class Lawrence Smith
    Airman 1st class Russell Pierson
    Airman 1st class Joseph Holcomb
    Airman 1st class Scott Camden

"Congratulations to all of you. I look forward to serving as your XO."

Then as Collins finished, Commander Jackson stood one last time to address the crew.

"I know you are already a great crew and now it's time to prove it. Over the last few days Lt. Commander Collins and I have been very pleased by your will power and self discipline to reach perfection as a team. Let us all strive to maintain the esprit de corps that has been exhibited to this point. God willing, in two days we will launch to Shepard Yard. The following day we'll begin our maiden voyage on the Pandora, but before that happens we have one little detail to attend to and gentlemen, I need your help.

"As you know it is customary for pilots to have a fitting call sign, and Mr. Collins has just informed me that every Pandora pilot has an appropriate call sign except one. So to that end and while it's just 'family' here tonight, I want to ask for suggestions from the Vindicator pilots for a proper call sign for Captain Starr, bearing in mind she'll be flying in space now, not just a fighter pilot. Now, who wants to throw out the first nomination?"

Quickly Captain Williams' hand shot into the air, and as he looked at Verna he said, "How about 'NAG' sir, as in, 'Not a guy'?" The reference drew one or two chuckles, but no reaction from Verna.

Commander Jackson said, "Judging by the crew's reaction to seeing her in full dress uniform, I think it's pretty clear to everyone that she is not a guy." But then he looked at Verna and asked, "What do you think, Captain?"

Verna just rolled her eyes. "Hmmm. How about another one?"

Jackson continued, "Who's next?"

"How about 'Cheerleader' or 'Space Cadet' offered Captain Fuller, drawing more chuckles from the crew and a yawn from Verna, who now appeared completely bored by all of it.

Then just as Commander Jackson was about to make his own suggestion, a strong, gravelly voice from the rear entrance of the cafeteria spoke up and asked, "How about, *'Rocket Babe'*?"

The crew had been watching Starr's reaction to the suggestions, and as they saw her jump to her feet in reaction to a familiar voice, they turned to see who had joined them. But before anyone could ask, as Verna ran toward him, she yelled, "Major Norris!"

Verna hugged him and whispered, "It's good to see you, sir!"

"It's good to see you too, Rookie."

As she and the Major walked toward him, Commander Jackson finally recognized Norris and invited him to come to the front. "Have a seat, Major Norris, and tell us what brings you here."

"Well, Commander, I'm just here to see my star student launch in a few hours, but when I heard the less than respectful suggestions for a call sign, well, I had to speak up."

"Is that so?" replied Jackson.

"Yes, sir, seeing how we all know she can out fly any man in this room. Knowing her proficiency with rockets, both flown and used as weapons, and from what I hear about her performance in defeating an F-15 recently on only one engine, not to mention her physical attributes, I thought something more fitting her talents, beauty, and achievements is justified."

"I see," Jackson said. "But I thought even you still call her Rookie. Isn't that right?"

"That's right. I gave her that call sign, but it was for a different time and not out of disrespect, and while I understand I'm not part of your little group, I think my suggestion will hold up with an honest crew, especially one that sites Semper Fi as one of its mottos."

"Fair enough," Jackson said. "Let's put it to the pilots and see what they think. You've all heard Major Norris's suggestion for Starr's call sign. What say ye?"

Major Knowles conferred a few moments with his pilots, and then looked directly at Commander Jackson. "Sir! As CAG, I wish to inform you that we unanimously agree and confirm Captain Starr's new call sign shall be 'Rocket Babe!'"

Jackson stood for a good 10 seconds before saying a word, then turned to Mr. Collins and ordered, "XO, please note for ship's roster: CAG has confirmed Captain Starr's call sign as '*Rocket Babe.*'"

The confirmation was followed by a very loud, "*Ooo Rah,*" from Captain Johns and his Marines.

Norris broke a slight grin and winked at Verna. "Now, how's that call sign suit you, Rookie?"

She smiled back and answered, "Right down to the ground, sir."

Chapter 7

Finally, New Year's Eve 1981 had arrived. Training was over, preparations were complete, and the crew was anxious to begin the mission. Every man and woman had made their final call to family to say good bye, and just before 2200 hours they boarded a single bus that took them to their destiny. Sounding very much like a high school class on a senior field trip, the bus was noisy and filled with excitement. Everyone was in a good mood.

Out at Launch Complex 39, Columbia and Challenger stood on pads A and B waiting to take the Pandora crew to the Shepard Yard. The crew arrived at exactly 2200 hours and as they drove up to the main gate, the bus suddenly went silent as they all saw a pair of glistening white shuttles bathed in spot lights. Verna was the first one to step down from the bus, and as she did she began to smile at the awe inspiring sight.

Major Knowles followed her off the bus, walked over to her and asked, "Are you excited to finally be going on the mission, Captain?"

Grinning from ear to ear, Verna turned to him and smiled, "Yes sir, absolutely. It has been a long time coming. This is the most exciting thing I have ever done."

"I do admire your childlike enthusiasm for everything you do, Verna. I only hope you still have it, if and when we return."

"We'll return, sir. All you have to do is keep the faith."

Major Knowles looked up at the moon, took a deep breath and said, "I hope it's that simple. I really do. You know, I've been meaning to pay you a visit the last couple of weeks to get caught up on how you've been doing since I last saw you but training has been so hectic and non-stop, there just hasn't been time."

"I know what you mean, sir, but I think we'll have a few minutes after we suit up. Once you are cleared for launch, come find me and we'll talk."

"That's a great idea. I'll see you in a few minutes."

Reaching the "suit up room" the crew began the arduous task of getting into their launch gear. For the men it was tedious and time consuming but for Verna it would turn out to be a piece of cake. As she entered her dressing room she was greeted by a very pleasant woman who introduced herself as Sharon and said that she was there to assist her any way possible.

"I'm sure you are aware the suits have to be air tight and they don't breathe like the normal uniforms you are used to wearing. The fabric tends to stick to bare skin as you pull it on."

"I understand," Verna said. "I had that problem on my first flight."

Sharon handed her a small box and said, "Well, there is an easy way to prevent all of that and be much more comfortable in the suit."

"Wonderful!" Verna said. "How do I do that?"

"It's easy;" she said. "You just wear pantyhose. You'll slide right in and the hose will act like a lubricant, making your movement much easier as you work. The men should do this too but they won't. Something about 'real men don't wear pantyhose.' You know how men can be."

Verna nodded then wriggled into the pantyhose as suggested and was able to ease into her suit in mere seconds. "Hey, this feels pretty good. I like it! It's a custom fit."

"Great," Sharon said with relief. "I'm glad. I got your medical records and measurements from the doctor so I could make a couple of minor alterations before you arrived, and I must say, you look amazing! Perhaps I should make one for myself. Take a look in the mirror, Captain, and see how you like it."

Verna pulled her boots on and walked over to a full length mirror, hoping to not look too fat. She looked hard and long before finally saying, "Thank you. It's perfect! I mean, wow! This is very nice!"

"Do you really think so, Captain?"

"Yes, yes I do. I couldn't have done better myself. You have a natural talent. It's very similar to the flight suit I made; almost like a cat suit, and it's black! I may just wear this out to dinner when I get back. If I didn't know better I'd say it was leather spandex. It's just so light and comfortable and really fits close!"

"I'm glad you approve, Captain. I worked very hard to make it just right for you since you will be wearing it most of the time."

"Your efforts are greatly appreciated, Sharon, and I will make sure the guys at the top know about this. What is your full name?"

"I'm Sharon Tucker. I designed and fabricated your suit."

"Well, no wonder it fits like a glove. Rest assured, you will get an excellent report from me!"

Just as she was about to leave there was a firm knock at the door. Sharon opened it to find Major Knowles ready to go and standing in the hall. "Looks like you have a visitor, Captain. Should I allow him in?"

"It depends," Verna said. "Does he have the keys to the Columbia?"

"I don't think so. He looks like a passenger to me."

Verna came to the door and smiled. "Come on in, Mike."

As soon as Sharon had left, Verna looked at Major Knowles and said, "Hey, you look good all dressed in black. I take it black is the color of choice now for DSSF."

"Could be," he answered. "Everyone else is in black as well, but it could also be that black shows less dirt. I don't know. I just put on what they gave me; no questions asked."

Verna smiled and agreed, "I guess we all do. Well, now that you're here, tell me what you have been up to since I last saw you."

Major Knowles told her all he had been doing since she was at JSC and how he came to be a part of the crew. It was all very interesting but Verna had been down this road before and finally asked him what he really wanted to know. He laughed and said, "Am I really that transparent?"

"Pretty much," she chortled. "This is not my first rodeo and we have known each other too long for you to be able to sneak anything by me. I have a pretty good idea what you want to know, so just ask."

"Ok, ok. This is off the record, and you know you don't have to answer if you would rather not. I'm not a doctor and I'm not here to do a psych evaluation, but as CAG of the Pandora, it's my job to know everything about my pilots, and I would like to ask you something very personal."

"That's fine, Mike. You know you can ask me anything. What is it?"

"Well, I was just wondering if you are still involved with that 'Indian?'"

"Oh yes, very much so."

"Are the two of you still in love?"

"Yes. Absolutely and without question!"

"Excellent," he said. "That's good to know."

"Yep. Everything in my love life is on course and rock steady. Why do you ask?"

"Well, to be honest, I was just wondering why he is letting you go on this mission. Shouldn't you be getting married and having little Indians by now?"

Verna looked a little surprised by the question, and then she exploded with laughter. "Why is he…'letting me go'? Is that what you asked me? He isn't letting me go. You know me better than that. He wants me to do what I have always dreamed of and that's pilot a spacecraft. As for little Indians, there's plenty of time for that when I get back. May I ask why you're concerned, Mike?"

"Sure. As you might imagine part of my job is to know that my pilots are mentally and emotionally sound; that they aren't distracted. And it is vitally important that they have the full support of their loved ones. I just wanted to make sure your loved ones are behind you 100%."

"Thank you for your concern, but I'm fine. I'm here with the full support of my parents and my soul mate."

"So you talked to him, and your mom and dad today?"

"Yes, I spoke to my parents and they think I'm going for more training at Shepard, that's all. As for Randy, he goes along with whatever I tell him without question."

"Well, that's fair enough," he said, "and good to know. I'm glad for you, but should you ever need a friend to talk to along the way, my door is always open."

Verna smiled and said, "I know Mike. You have always been a good friend to both of us. I'm just glad I will have another friend along for the ride. You and Bill Collins are the only friends I have making this little trip to the Red Planet. Maybe the three of us can play a game or two of chess along the way."

"Really? Will there be chess on the Pandora?"

"Sure, Mike. Electronic… on the computer."

"That's depressing," he said. "Nearly 28 billion dollars for a ship and all they can do is electronic chess; not even a real chess set. It's sad really." Then glancing at his watch he said, "It's almost time to board. We need to catch up with the others."

As they approached the loading zone they could hear Collins calling out who was assigned to which shuttle. To keep it simple the bridge crew and airmen would be going up on Columbia with Commander Jackson, while the rest would be riding up on Challenger with Collins. When Collins had finished with his announcements, Jackson asked him if he knew the whereabouts of the co-pilot and CAG, but as he did his question was muffled by a chorus of whistles and cheers coming from behind him as Knowles and Starr came down the ramp to the bus. One of the Marines yelled "Look, it's Emma Peel!"

Another yelled, "No, it's Cat Woman!"

Then a third yelled, "It's *Rocket Babe!*" and at that point all the men except for Jackson formed a corridor for her that led to the bus, and as she walked through they all began to chant, "*Rocket Babe! Rocket Babe! Rocket Babe!*"

Commander Jackson let them go for a few seconds then looked at Collins and said, "I think that's enough. Call it."

At that point Mr. Collins yelled as loud as he could, "AT EASE!" Not really knowing what to think of it all, Verna turned to face Commander Jackson and stood at attention. Collins slowly walked over to her and whispered, "I said *at ease*. Relax. Oh, and by the way, nice flight suit!" Collins smiled at her and then told them all to board the bus.

With everyone ready to go the driver radioed mission control to let them know they were ready to proceed, and as he began rolling the lights went out all over the base. Even the shuttles went dark. After a moment Major Knowles leaned over to Collins and said, "Sir if I didn't know better I would almost think they didn't want anyone to know what we're doing."

Collins chuckled, "You mean because we are all dressed in black, the bus is black and the base is under black out conditions?"

"Something like that," he answered. "It's going to make it hard for anyone to see us boarding. What's Ivan going to think?"

"Well, Major, it's probably not the first time Ivan has been left in the dark and it most likely won't be the last."

Knowles nodded in agreement and assured him, saying, "Not if we have anything to say about it."

Two hours later the base was back to normal with both shuttles loaded and ready for their night launch. While the flight crew was going through their prelaunch checklists, all anyone else could do was wait to see if they were a go or a no go. There was room enough in the shuttle cabins for up to seven people to fit comfortably, but for the twelve men strapped into make shift seats in the cargo bays, it was a long wait. As far as the media knew there were only three men on each shuttle, taking more building materials to Shepard Yard for construction of a future space station.

Outside the shuttles, a clear, moonless sky awaited illumination from the first ever dual shuttle launch, as twin count downs proceeded only 20 seconds apart. If all went well, Columbia would launch first at exactly 0500 with Challenger following close behind.

The minutes dragged by until they were at T minus 3 minutes in the countdown, then they heard Mission Control say… "Network, we need a final launch status check…"

OTC -Go!

TBC - Go!

FIDO - Go!

Guidance — Go!

Surgeon - Go!

LPS - Go!

Houston Flight - Go!

STM — Go!

Safety Console - Go!

STE — Go!

CDR - Go!

Payload manager - Go!

Range Weather - Go!

Security - Go! F15's on station have cleared a 1,000 mile radius.

SRO - The range is clear to launch.

"Launch Director, launch team is ready to proceed. Columbia, you are cleared to launch at T-minus 90 seconds and counting."

"Acknowledged. Columbia standing by for launch."

After a short pause, SDF pilot and Shuttle Commander, Jake Cole, came over the internal com-line. "Pandora crew, we are go for launch. Just sit back, enjoy the ride and we'll deliver you to Shepard Yard shortly."

Strapped in on the lower deck, Verna glanced at Commander Jackson and said, "I wish I at least had a window seat. This monitor is too small to see any real detail of the launch."

Jackson shook his head and then replied, "Come on now, Captain. Just say it. Wouldn't you really rather be flying Columbia yourself?"

"Well… yes sir, I would. But I got stuck here in 2nd class. I suppose it's better than being left behind."

"That's an excellent point, Captain. Try and remember that."

"T minus 60 seconds and counting. Transferring to orbiter internal power. Columbia is now running on its three onboard fuel cells. Coming up on a go for auto sequence start.…We are go for auto sequence start. Columbia's computers have primary control.

"T minus 15 seconds and counting.… 12 ,11, 10, 9, 8, 7, 6…"The crew felt and heard the rumble of the 3 main engines beginning to start up… 5, 4… At 3 seconds all three orbiter engines were up and running, and the crew felt a slight upward motion as the orbiter lifted a few inches just prior to release from the pad … 2, 1, booster ignition… and liftoff! *We have liftoff of Columbia, returning to ShepardYard as we continue to pave the way toward manned exploration of the solar system!*"

Seven seconds later Columbia executed its roll program and continued to rapidly rise into the night sky riding a pillar of fire and smoke that could be seen for hundreds of miles. Everyone on board could feel the orbiter shaking and baking her way to thinner atmosphere, as they were all pinned into their seats.

Shortly after Columbia completed her roll program, back on Pad 39 B Challenger came to life and roared into the night sky. Things happened rapidly during this phase of the launch. Columbia throttled back to 67 % until she was past max Q - maximum dynamic pressure. After a few seconds more they heard, "Columbia you are go for throttle up."

"Roger. Go for throttle up." And then her main engines went back to 104 %. To this point all was going well and the ride became very smooth. At two minutes and three seconds, the SRB's were jettisoned and Columbia had 6 minutes to main engine cut off.

Now, most of the crew was unusually quiet. A few were nervous and trying not to let it show. Starr was very excited and smiling like a Cheshire cat as she tried to see anything other than black sky on the monitor, but she wasn't having much luck. All along the way they could hear CAPCOM giving updates for various aborts, the first being "negative return." Then after a few minutes and passing each abort point in the launch, Starr finally heard the call she had been waiting for: "Columbia, press to MECO."

"Roger CAPCOM. Press to MECO." Not long after, Columbia's engines shutdown and the main tank was jettisoned.

"Yes!" Verna said under her breath. "We're doing great! Flawless!"

All the way and only 5 miles behind, Challenger was mimicking every move of Columbia and she also performed flawlessly. To this point it had been the greatest launch day in the history of the space program and as fate would have it, it would be the only occasion that two shuttles were launched at the same time or carried live personnel in the cargo bays.

As Columbia held true, Challenger executed a slightly longer burn to MECO that allowed her to catch up with Columbia, and from there the two flew in formation all the way to Shepard. Over the next 14 hours the passengers of Columbia and Challenger spent their time getting used to a weightless environment and enjoying the view, the most inspiring of which came as they approached their destination. Shepard Yard was impressive enough all on its own but seeing the Pandora for the first time left them all speechless. Not a sound was heard until Commander Cole broke the silence. "Attention. We will begin docking procedure in 5 minutes. Please return to your seats and strap in. Our approach will be visible on your monitors and you may listen in over your headphones."

"Shepard Yard, this is Columbia requesting permission to dock."

"Columbia, permission granted. You are cleared for docking at starboard Portal 1."

"Roger, Shepard. Lining up on Portal 1." Then with the steady hand of a brain surgeon, Commander Cole patiently guided Columbia to a very gentle and perfect capture.

"Shepard and Houston, Columbia shows capture."

"Roger Columbia. Shepard confirms capture. Great job!"

In just a moment Commander Cole was back on the com-line. "Pandora crew, please make your way to the portal in the order you are seated and proceed to main habitat."

Glad to be docked and headed for their own ship, the crew made their way to and through the portal as quickly as they could. Just as Starr was about to take her turn out the door she stopped long enough to speak to Commander Cole. "Thanks for a great flight, Jake, and a most impressive capture. I didn't even feel contact."

Cole smiled broadly and said, "It was my pleasure, Verna. Good to see you again. Good luck with your mission. I'll be here to take you home when you return."

"I'm going to hold you to it," she replied. Then she went into the tunnel with Jackson close behind.

When they were finally standing on the main habitat deck, Commander Jackson asked her how she knew Commander Cole. "You mean, Jake? Oh, he and I go way back, all the way to Homestead. The first time I was involved in war games there, he was my first kill… and my fifth… and my eleventh, and he was here at Shepard for a month when I went through Vindicator training. I think he kind of had a crush on me back then."

"You seem to know a lot of people, Captain. Just how many people in DSSF do you know?"

"Of the 3,000 officially serving, I know 1,627, sir."

"Would I be correct in assuming you know everything about them, Captain?"

"Only what's in their dossier, sir."

"Would I also be correct in assuming that you mean word for word?"

"Yes, sir, word for word."

"How do you do that?"

"Eidetic memory, sir. We talked about that at our first meeting, remember?" After a moment or two to consider her answer, Jackson started to ask her another question but then just shook his head in disbelief and told her to follow him.

The stay at Shepard would be brief. Once the crew of the Pandora had been reunited, they were fed and then taken to their quarters, basically a large room that had a lot of hooks on the wall where they would sleep, more or less, in a sack hanging from the wall. Major Driskill looked around the room and moaned, "Man, when they say hit the sack, they aren't kidding!"

Verna nodded her head, and laughed. "There's nothing like standard issue."

Commander Jackson told them all to find a place and get some sleep. "In eight hours we will transfer to the Pandora and begin preflight for launch."

As the lights dimmed Verna found an empty "sack," secured it to the wall, and removed only her boots before snuggling in for the night. It wasn't exactly a Magic Fingers massage mattress, but it would do. Once she had stretched out, she began to float horizontal to the floor and was soon fast asleep.

Across the room, two of the airmen found themselves having a hard time getting to sleep. It was their first trip into space and after a few minutes of tossing about, they looked at each other and then at Starr quietly dreaming away. "It must be nice," one man said. "How did she get to sleep so fast? This is just crazy. I need to feel something solid under me."

Captain Johns asked, "How about I bounce your skulls against a bulkhead? Would that be solid enough for you? Shut up and get some sleep, grunts!"

"Yes sir," they replied, and from that point on, no one said a word.

Verna woke seven hours later to the smell of coffee; KONA coffee! The moment that aroma made it to her olfactory her eyes snapped open like a chute behind a fighter on landing. "Kona! I smell Kona!" Faster than you could say Rip Van Winkle she was out of her sack, into her boots and following her nose down the hall. "It's getting stronger... stronger... there it is!" she cried, as a pot encircled by what appeared to be a child's sippy cup came into view. "I know they have to have lids but I simply hate these cups," she said to herself.

Quickly she filled a cup to the brim and tasted it. "Yes! Yes! Yes!" As she looked around the room she saw Collins sitting at a table bolted to the floor. Seeing him sitting there grinning at her she blared, "You lied! You said they wouldn't have Kona up here but they do!"

"No, ma'am, I didn't lie. They don't have Kona... but I do. Mary asked me to bring a can for you."

"I should have known," she said. "Only a woman would be that thoughtful, but I will give you half credit for bringing it up."

"Half credit? Do you know what I had to do to get a single can of that *black-nitro* on board?"

"Whatever it was, it was worth it, and thank you both! Now, where's the rest of it?"

"Why? You can't brew it on Pandora."

"Ohhh yes, I can. I brought some, too, and I had a little talk with Chief Engineer Driskill yesterday. He said he'll have a pot in engineering anytime I want it!"

"Do you make friends everywhere you go, Captain?"

"Yes, actually, I do."

Collins smiled and said, "I suppose it is good to have friends in high places."

Verna laughed and said, "It's good to have them in low places, too. I have the Kona, Driskill has a pot, sounds like friends to me. Hey, it kind of makes you wonder what else has been smuggled aboard, doesn't it?"

He thought about it a minute, then said, "No, I don't want to wonder. I want to be like Shultz. I know nut-zing! Nut-zing! If I know, I'm supposed to tell Commander Jackson, so don't tell me anything else."

"Fine by me. I won't tell you anything."

"Well, you can tell me one thing."

"What's that?" she asked.

"Why don't these chairs float around like everything else here? The table is bolted to the floor, but the chairs aren't."

"Well, Bill, if I tell you, you have to keep it to yourself."

"Ok, I will. Now tell me."

"You won't tell Commander Jackson?"

"No, I won't tell Commander Jackson!"

"Ok then… I'll tell you… and as she burst out laughing she said, "They're magnetic!" Collins got up, gave her a sour look and walked away while she continued laughing. "You're a hoot, Bill!"

A few seconds later they heard Westminster Chimes coming over the P.A. system and not long after, they were joined by the rest of the crew as they lurched their way into the mess hall. There was just enough time for them to eat, dress and saddle up.

Chapter 8

At 0800, January 1, 1982, 32 men and one woman boarded the Pandora for the very first time. Each one stored their gear, then found their duty stations exactly as practiced on the Pandora mock-up. Commander Jackson was the last one to step through the airlock and Airman Camden closed and secured the hatch behind him. As Jackson stepped onto the bridge for the first time, he paused a moment to look around the room and enjoy the view.

Looking up from his console, communications officer Lt. Ryan loudly proclaimed, "Commander on deck!" As those present stood to attention, Ryan pulled an old style boson whistle from his pocket and piped Jackson aboard.

Seeing the whistle, Jackson smiled at Ryan and commended him, "Nice touch, son. Glad to see you're 'old school.' I hate that synthesized garbage."

"Yes sir. Old school, sir!"

The young lieutenant's enthusiasm caused the commander to chuckle a bit as he replied, "At ease, Ryan. Save some of that enthusiasm for the trip."

Jackson looked at Starr and asked, "Great day for a launch isn't it, Captain?"

"I believe so, sir, but could I have a moment?"

"Now, Captain?"

"Just a moment, sir."

"Well, hurry up!"

Because Commander Jackson was a good ten inches taller, Verna motioned for him to lean down so she could whisper in his ear, "There's something wrong with Connor, sir."

"What are you implying, Captain?"

"He's too edgy sir; like he's had way too much coffee."

"Oh, he's probably just excited to be launching. Aren't you excited, Captain?"

"Yes, of course, but it's more than that. He seems agitated, anxious, and much more so than a man with his experience should be."

Jackson hesitated for a moment, and then said, "I don't know, Captain. He looks fine to me. What would you have me do, abort the launch?"

"No sir. Just reporting what I'm seeing."

"Your concern is noted, but for now get strapped in. We only have a few seconds before launch. Unless you have something concrete, we'll proceed with the countdown."

"Your call, sir."

Starr went to the copilot's chair, sat down and began to buckle in. As she did Connor noticed she was mumbling under her breath.

"What are you on about, Captain?" barked Connor.

"Excuse me?" came the reply.

"What is that you're mumbling about?"

"Oh, nothing sir. Just thinking out loud.

"Well, it's very annoying. Keep it to yourself and pay attention!"

"Oh, yes sir!"

Seeing all bridge stations manned and ready, Jackson checked the forward and aft view screens then strapped himself in. After a long hard look at Connor he said, "Gentlemen, prepare to launch Pandora. XO, give me a roll call and launch status. Check with Shepard and Pandora."

"Aye, sir! Roll call and launch status check."

Starr leaned over and whispered to Connor, "Didn't we just do this?"

"I believe so, but here we go again."

"Shepard, Pandora requesting launch status check."

"Pandora, launch status check on your command…"
"FIDO - Go!"
"Guidance - Go!"
"INCO - Go!"
"Surgeon - Go!"
"LPS - Go!"
"Houston Flight - Go!"
"Shepard Flight - Go!"
"STM - Go!"
"Safety Console - Go!"
"CAPCOM - Go!"
"Security - Go!"
"SRO - Pandora cleared to launch."
"Pandora, Shepard is go!"
"Roger, Shepard, please stand by."
"Pandora crew, this is the XO. Roll call and launch status check, now!
"Engineering – Driskill, all systems nominal. Engineering is go!"
"CAG – Knowles, Launch Bays and Vindicators secure, 101st Combat Wing locked and loaded. We are go!"
"Medical – Patel. Medical is go!"
"Communications – Ryan. Go!"
"Command Pilot – Connor. Go!"
"Co-Pilot – Starr. Go!"
"Flight Engineer – Fontaine. Go!"
"Commander, Shepard and all Pandora stations reporting go! Crew secure and ready for launch."
"Thank you, Mr. Collins. Commander acknowledges go status. Shepard, Pandora standing by to launch."
"Mr. Ryan, give me ship wide."
"You have ship wide, sir."
"All personnel, this is the commander. Set launch conditions

throughout the ship. Mr. Connor, pressurize all tanks. Standby to cast off. Starr, activate ion shield now."

"Aye sir. Shield... at 100%."

"Flight engineer says Pandora is go!"

"Shepard, Pandora shows pressurization complete. Ready to release all moorings."

"Roger, Pandora. Prepare to release on my mark: 3... 2...1 mark!"

At the moment the moorings retracted, Connor performed a two second RCS burn that pushed the Pandora down and away from Shepard in a belly first free fall and toward launch position.

"Pandora, begin two minute countdown to ignition... now!"

"Roger, Shepard. Countdown, start."

All over the ship the crew watched the clock tick down on their monitors, each one anxious to get underway. Approximately 300 feet behind the bridge and strapped in tight, Major Driskill looked at Major Knowles and his pilots and commented, "I think this is it, men."

"Looks like it," Knowles responded. "About time, too! I was getting tired of waiting."

"Yeah, I know what you mean. There are only so many times you can run a systems check before you go stir crazy."

"Tell me about it. I've run so many checks on the Vindicators I can do it in my sleep."

Their monitor was now showing T minus 12 seconds and counting as they heard the valves start to open on the fuel tanks and the F-1 bells begin to gimbal. Knowles looked at Driskill and said, "That's a lot of creaking. I didn't think we'd be able to hear anything in here."

Driskill half way shook his head in agreement before explaining, "If we were outside or a little further forward, we couldn't hear a thing, but this far aft with plenty of steel and air to conduct the sound, it's not a problem. Don't let it worry you. Just wait until the engines fire up. You'll be glad you have that helmet to muffle the sound. All five engines will start at 20% but as soon as they have guidance confirmed, they'll punch it up to 60% for a few seconds then 100% until we reach cruising speed. Just hang on until the noise stops and pray there are no problems."

"You can count on the prayers, Major!"

"Good. I'll get back to you later. I have to monitor this board until we reach MECO. Enjoy the launch!"

Back on the Bridge, Commander Jackson watched Major Connor and Starr set the switches and dials on their consoles, as the clock wound down… "10… 9… guidance now internal, 8… 7… 6, ignition sequence start 5… 4… 3 we have ignition on all five engines, 2… 1… we have a launch! All 5 engines are running at 20% and Pandora has cleared the yard!"

As the crew began to sink deep into their seats, at 10 seconds into the flight and for no apparent reason, Connor flipped the controls to manual and nudged the stick forward but didn't feel a response at first. Suddenly he began to feel strange as he became light headed and his vision blurred. Fighting to maintain control of himself, he could tell by the monitor that the ship was still in free fall but he could not detect any forward motion or the passing of time. Then after another second or two a feeling of complete panic came over him. Connor looked at Starr and saw her right hand on her stick. He looked angry and yelled, "*Let it go!*"

"What?"

"Let it go! Stop working against me!"

"What's wrong?"

"Let go of your stick!"

"I'm not doing anything. You have it, sir."

"Move your hand; *now!*"

"Yes sir," and with that Starr placed her hands in her lap.

Commander Jackson leaned forward and loudly asked, "What's wrong, Connor?"

"I don't know, sir. We're just free falling. We're not moving forward!"

"Yes, we are," Starr interjected.

"No, we are not, Captain! We're still falling straight into the atmosphere."

"No sir, look at the instruments. We're fine. Why did you disengage autopilot? We're exactly where we should be: eight miles down range at 1,600 mph and rapidly increasing speed!"

Instead of answering her question, all at once Connor panicked and pushed the throttles to 80%, accelerating the ship past its design limits for this early in the launch. "No, sir!" Starr yelled. "Back off! Back off! We can't exceed 20% until we're at least 60 seconds into the flight. Stay at or under 4 G's, max! Give her a chance to get her bearings!" But it was too late. Connor's knee jerk reaction created a problem with the gyro controlling the number three engine, causing it to oscillate from side to side. "Don't you feel that?" Starr screamed. "One of the engines is trying to gimbal into position. Back off and let it catch up."

Connor snapped back, "You don't know everything, Captain. I'm the Command Pilot. We'll do it my way!"

The main board in engineering lit up like a Christmas tree. "What…in…the…world??" yelled Major Knowles.

"It seems the tail is wagging the dog," Driskill answered. "If I didn't know better I'd say we have a wayward engine…"

"Yep, looks like number three gyro is having a problem. If they don't do it in the next few seconds, I'm going to see if I can shut it down from here." Driskill's fingers were a blur as he frantically tried to send a command that would shut down the confused engine but it was not responding. All over the ship soldiers hung on for dear life and prayed for divine intervention. Telemetry to Shepard was cutoff as the main antenna line blew a breaker due to all the vibration and CAPCOM had no idea what was happening.

When Ryan saw the red light on his console come on he announced to the bridge, "We've lost main communication with Shepard." Meanwhile

Shepard and Houston were frantically trying to re-establish the link.

"Shepard? Houston. We've lost telemetry but we believe the problem is on the ship."

"Roger, Houston. Everything here checks out. Our radar shows a slightly erratic flight path and thrust, but that's all we can tell. They're still under power and generally on course."

Connor's hand held steady as the oscillations grew worse. With her hands still in her lap, Starr pleadingly looked at Commander Jackson and shouted, "If he keeps this up we're all going to die!"

Jackson only hesitated for a moment then said, "Let her help you, Connor."

"I'm the command pilot, sir! I will not be told how to fly by a little girl."

"But you will do what I tell you," Jackson roared. "Major Connor, you are relieved as command pilot! Starr, take control of Pandora!"

"Gladly, sir!"

Quickly looking over her tactical display, Verna informed Jackson "Sir, I only have partial control. We have to carefully shut everything down to regain full control."

"*Do it now!*" Jackson ordered.

Verna quickly and smoothly managed to reduce power to 10% on all five engines, but try as she might number three would not shutdown completely. "Engine three seems to be locked at 10%, and one degree off center, sir. If I shut down all the others and number three keeps running, we'll go into a huge arc. As they are now, the other four engines are over riding number three's effect."

Verna looked at Ryan and said, "I need to talk to Driskill."

Ryan flipped a switch then nodded, "You're on, Captain."

"Major Driskill, this is Starr. I believe we need to shut down all five engines at the same time to regain control, but the engines are not fully responding to me on the bridge. I need your help in engineering."

"Agreed," Driskill replied. I'm way ahead of you. I think if we both send a command to shutdown at the same time, they will all respond. I'm already set up. Just tell me when."

"There's no time like the present, Major, in 3, 2, 1, now!" Then, with the command to shut down coming from the bridge and engineering, all five engines stopped instantly. "Yes!" Verna shouted. "Major Driskill, please stand by while I recalculate our course."

"Nice work, Captain. Engineering standing by."

Having sat quietly since Starr took over, Connor asked her if she wanted to use his slide rule. "Not for this," she said. "I can do it in my head." After a few seconds Verna had input the corrected data and told Commander Jackson that she was ready to restart.

"Excellent, Captain. What's our status?"

"We are currently two degrees off course and holding at 7,153 mph. I have programmed the course correction and speed to put us back where we should be and on time."

Recognizing the look on her face, Jackson reluctantly asked, "But.... what, Captain?"

"I'd like to put her on manual, sir."

"Manual?"

"Yes, sir. Manual."

Collins looked at Jackson and began to smile. Jackson pretended not to see Collins but after a few seconds and sounding frustrated he agreed. "I'm not even going to ask why, Captain... Permission granted." Verna spun around in her seat with a huge smile on her face and reached for the stick.

"Ryan, give me ship wide."

"You have ship wide, Commander."

"Ok, boys and girls, we're going to try it again. Hold on, and hold your breath. Captain Starr has your life in her hands. At your leisure, Captain."

"Major Driskill, this is Starr. Are you ready?"

"Engineering is go! Tanks are pressurized, all systems show nominal and number one RTG is dedicated to start up."

"Acknowledged, sir. Ignition... now!" Starr eased the throttles forward and pushed the big green button. The entire ship felt the engines come to life, and after a few seconds she reported their status. "Engineering, I'm showing all five engines at 20%; gyros in complete control."

"Engineering confirms: 20 % and all engines nominal."

"My board shows green, Major."

"Confirmed, Captain. Engineering shows green and you may want to speak up a bit. It's kind of noisy down here right now."

"Roger, Major. I'll try to speak up."

"What's the duration on the burn?" Jackson asked.

"We'll go 60 seconds at 20%, 30 seconds at 60%. Then if all goes well, I'll push her to the wall for 215 seconds. That will get us to exactly 24,500 mph."

"Don't you mean approximately 24,500, Captain?"

"No, sir, I mean exactly 24,500."

"Collins looked at him and said, "Remember when you were talking to the President and I tried to tell you not to call HQ? Well, this is one of those times, sir."

"Ah... I see. Thank you, Mr. Collins."

As Pandora resumed powered flight, Shepard and Houston were completely bewildered by what they were seeing. "Shepard? Houston. As best we can tell they shut down for a few moments but now they're back up and running... and seem to be straight and true."

"Roger, Houston. We see it but com-link is still down. We have no idea what's going on."

Back on Pandora... "Engineering, we're approaching 60 seconds and throttle up."

"Roger, Captain. Engineering shows go for first throttle up."

Verna eased the controls forward evenly to 60% and barely moved the stick to either side as she watched Pandora's speed increase in huge chunks. "Just keep the little green dot between the red lines. That's all we need," she said to herself.

"Captain, engineering showing nominal at 60%. In 10 seconds you're go for 104%."

"Roger that, engineering."

As promised, Verna gently pushed all five engines to max power and again Pandora responded smoothly and without hesitation. After a few more seconds Verna began calling out their speed at 20 second intervals. "Speed now exceeding 15k…18k…21k. Engineering, stand by for MECO. Speed now at 23,000… 24,000… MECO… now!" Starr cut power to the engines and without any drama whatsoever they all shutdown.

"Engineering confirms MECO."

Starr swiveled her seat sideways to look at Jackson and announced, "Pandora dead on course, back on schedule, and cruising at exactly 24,500 mph, sir! Returning Pandora to autopilot."

Jackson smiled slightly and said, "Nicely done, Captain. I am… impressed." Then he looked at Collins who was also smiling broadly and very quietly told Collins to remind him to send a short thank you note to Major Norris… "…if we make it back home."

Collins nodded, "Without question sir, I will remind you."

Then he turned to Ryan and said, "Put me through to medical."

"Aye, sir."

"Patel here. How may I help you?"

"Doctor, Connor is on his way to see you. Check him over and get back to me ASAP."

"What, exactly, am I looking for?"

"I'm not sure. He wasn't himself during launch and I want him checked out."

"Yes, sir, ASAP."

"Mr. Connor, do you require assistance getting to medical?"

"No, sir. I can make it."

"Then report there immediately."

"Yes, sir."

"That's strange," Ryan said. "Communications with Houston and telemetry are back on line, sir, and I have CAPCOM standing by. Engineering to bridge."

"Yes, Mr. Driskill."

"The main dish is back on line, sir. It was just a breaker. All ship's systems now show 100%."

"Thank you, Mr. Driskill."

"Aye, sir. Driskill out."

"XO, secure from launch conditions. Ryan, inform CAG we need his best pilot up here on the double. Let Houston know we're alive and proceeding on course, then begin transmitting our flight recorder information to them and ask for a quick analysis of the launch. I want to know if it was all just Connor or something else."

"Aye, sir."

Suddenly Ryan let out a cheer and yelled, "Yes! I finally figured it out!"

His outburst nearly caused Collins to fall out of his seat. Spinning around in his chair Collins yelled back, "What did you figure out, Lieutenant?"

"I finally know how to turn off the stupid Quindar tone, sir! The constant beep, beep, beep was just about to drive me insane."

"I'm happy for you, son, but how about next time you discover something, don't announce it quite so loud!"

"Yes, sir. Sorry sir."

As Ryan spoke to Major Knowles, Verna turned around and said to Jackson, "That wasn't too bad for a little girl now, was it?"

Jackson thought a moment, and then said, "There are no little girls on the Pandora, Captain, only a Rocket Babe, and I know I'm probably going to regret this but I have to ask you just one question."

"What's that, sir?"

"Why is it that Connor couldn't fly the ship manually, but you could?"

Verna smiled wryly, "That's easy, sir. Major Connor's mistake was that he didn't understand the Pandora is a lady, and like most ladies, she only responds favorably to a 'light touch.' If he gets too demanding or tries to fly her again like she's a Corvette, there's going to be more trouble."

Jackson shook his head and mumbled, "I knew I was going to regret asking her."

Then she added, "I'm sure all Houston will find is that the Major didn't give the gyros enough time to align properly. There's nothing wrong with the ship, sir."

"Thank you for your diagnosis, Chief Engineer Starr! I hope you won't mind if I have Houston confirm your theory."

"It's their time to waste, sir. I guess there's no harm in a double check."

At that moment a rugged looking, 6 foot 3 inch, blonde haired, blue eyed pilot stepped onto the bridge. "Major DeArman reporting, sir."

Jackson glanced at him and said, "Assume the command pilot chair, Major."

Starr grinned and quietly said, "Welcome to first class, Emmett. Glad you could join us."

"Me too, Captain. I didn't think I would be on the bridge so soon."

"Didn't you know, Major? That's why being on the Pandora is so much fun. You never know what will happen next."

Ten minutes later Patel was calling to report on Connor. "Medical to bridge."

"Go ahead, Doctor."

"Commander, I've completed my exam of Major Connor. Over all, he is fine now, but his blood test indicates he has recently ingested what I believe to be a designer cocktail of alcohol, benzodiazepines and anabolic steroids. In other words, he was given a mickey. In the proper amount, any of those ingredients alone could cause him to be anxious or aggressive but all together they would certainly cause him to act irrationally until they worked their way out of his system."

"And how would he come by those drugs, doctor?"

"Judging by the level in his blood, he had to have gotten it this morning, most likely in his coffee. Couple it all with the stress of a first launch and it was just a little too much for him, but he will be fine."

"When can he return to duty?"

"Probably tomorrow, but for now I want him to drink plenty of fluids and get some rest."

"Sounds fine to me. Tell him to rest for 24 hours then report for second watch tomorrow."

"That should be fine, Commander."

"While I have you on line, doctor, how is the rest of the crew?"

"I would say in good shape. I have only had one person so far complain of motion sickness."

"Keep me informed, doctor."

"Acknowledged. Medical out."

"Finally!" Commander Jackson exclaimed. "Looks like all the brush fires are out."

"I believe so, sir," Starr replied. "My stat-board shows all stations nominal."

"Mr. Ryan, have you completed transmitting our launch data to Houston?"

"Yes, sir, just now."

"Good! Now, if Major DeArman is settled in, the XO and I would like to see Captain Starr in my quarters."

"Oh, I'm good to go, sir," DeArman said with a huge smile on his face. "Y'all take your time."

"In that case, Captain, if you will…"

Commander Jackson was the only person on board to have his own private quarters but with the three of them in there at the same time, the room seemed more like a holding cell than a commander's quarters. To call it Spartan would be a gross understatement. At first glance the 8 by 10 foot room appeared almost empty because all of the fixtures were recessed into the walls and folded out to save space. When the cot, sink, small table and 2 chairs were deployed, they took up 90% of the room.

"Nice," Collins smirked. "Should we take turns breathing, sir?"

Flipping down one of the chairs from the wall, Jackson stared at Collins, faked a smile and sarcastically asked, "Are you planning on going into stand-up comedy when we get back, Bill? Vegas, maybe? Why don't you pull up some deck and have a seat? Starr, flip down that black handle and sit over there."

Verna giggled and said, "Thank you, sir," as she sat on the other seat with her back to the wall.

Collins looked at her a second before complaining. "Oh, I see. I get to stand while you pretend to laugh at his jokes to get brownie points."

"No, it was actually funny. You should have seen the look on your face."

"Ok, that's enough, you two. Let's get down to business."

"Starr, you've told that you have an eidetic memory. Is that correct?"

"Yes, sir."

"Well, tell me, what exactly does that mean?"

"I could give you a lengthy text book definition, sir, but basically I have total recall of everything I have ever read, seen and experienced."

"When you say everything…"

"I mean everything, sir."

"Any and all past experiences and conversations?"

"Yes, sir."

"Is that so? May I take it then that you've read the specs on the Pandora as provided by our XO?"

"Yes, sir, I have."

"Would you mind giving me a little demonstration?"

"I would be happy to, sir."

Jackson picked up a three inch thick copy of the Pandora flight manual and said, "OK, then. I'm going to read along while you give me a quick rundown on Pandora."

"No problem, sir. Per the manual provided to me last week by Lt. Commander Collins, turn to page 2. Pandora: Juno Class Cestris Saturn V, 72 feet longer than the original Apollo era Saturn V. Increased power and efficiency comes from 5 of the new F-1D engines that provide 40% more thrust with a much longer impulse of 750 seconds. The interior redesign increased main fuel tank capacity to 6.6 million pounds. Pandora's general specifications are as follows: length 425 feet, average diameter 33 feet, Vindicator bays tip to tip 133 feet, 4,500 square feet of deck, each. Gross mass 8.5 million pounds, thrust 10.75 million pounds. Payload including crew and armament 405,000 pounds. Vindicators: 6. Standard crew: 33."

"Stop! That's enough, I'm convinced. You're a combination tape recorder and encyclopedia. How many manuals on Pandora's operations have you committed to memory, Captain?"

"Including armaments and Vindicators, there are 26 manuals total, pertaining to Pandora. I know them all, word for word, sir."

"What about DSSF regulations? Those, too?"

"Yes, sir."

"Can I rely on you to provide me with exact information, on demand, for any reason, issue, specification or regulation?"

"Always, sir."

"Excellent. I'm glad. I have to admit, Captain, that while I did not initially want you on the ship, I have quickly come to respect, and more importantly, trust you, and I cannot imagine Pandora without you now."

"Thank you, sir. I appreciate you saying that. I will work hard to show your trust is not misplaced and I must say sir, that while it is not required to perform my duties, it is nice to be accepted."

Jackson smiled at her like a father would his daughter and said, "They say you can't teach an old dog new tricks, Captain, but you have proven them and me wrong."

Meanwhile in engineering, Knowles and Driskill were completing preparations for the Vindicators to launch. "They're all fueled, armed, and ready to go, Mike."

"Thanks for your help, Major. If my pilots and I can be of assistance to you anytime, just let us know."

"No problem. I'd be glad to do it and I may take you up on your offer sooner than you think. Do you have anyone with experience on the manned maneuvering unit?"

"Sure. Starr and I both trained on the prototype. Why?"

"Well, I was just thinking, when we catch up with the supply ship, if the smaller items could be brought aboard that way, I could focus on swapping out the fuel modules and cut the transfer time in half."

"Sounds like fun to me. I'll do the MMU work. I always wanted a jet pack as a kid."

"That would be great, and make my job much easier. I'll even cut you in for some of Starr's Kona coffee when we're finished."

"Blake, do you have Kona?"

"No, sadly, I don't. Starr does." Then with a huge smile he bragged, "I have the pot."

"Ohhh, sounds like a party to me," Knowles agreed. "Too bad we don't have some sippin' whiskey to go with it. You know, just a touch."

"Oh, that's no problem, my friend. The XO has that."

"Well then, we'll have to invite him, too."

"Yes, sir! Definitely going be a party in engineering! Come on, supply ship!"

Chapter 9

Two days into the flight Commander Jackson was looking out the port window of the bridge when he asked Starr for an ETA on the supply ship. "We will overtake it in 1 hour, 16 minutes, 22 seconds, sir, and once we're refueled, we can stop puttering around."

"Puttering around?" Jackson inquired. "Do you really consider 24,500 mph puttering, Captain?"

"Well, sir, in a ship with the potential to break 100,000 mph, yes sir, we're practically idling."

Jackson paused a moment then quietly commented to her, "There are times, Captain, that you actually scare me. Tell me, Captain, once we complete resupply maneuvers, how long to Mars?"

"Currently Mars is still close to 34 million miles away, but as you know, our flight plan calls for us to increase speed to 60,000 mph once refueling is complete. If we stay within the 90 minutes allotted for resupply and the burn goes as planned, from that point we will arrive at Mars in 23.61 days or twelve-thirty one hours, January 26."

Mr. Ryan confirmed, "I'm picking up the short range beacon from the supply ship, sir."

"Good! Notify engineering to prepare for resupply."

"Aye sir. Bridge to engineering. Prepare for resupply rendezvous in approximately one hour."

"Engineering acknowledged. Is Commander Jackson available?"

"Jackson here. What can I do for you, Major Driskill?"

"Sir, I'd like to request permission for Major Knowles to assist me with resupply by using the MMU."

"I don't recall the MMU being a part of that operation, Major."

"It's not, sir, but he is agreeable and it would cut our resupply operation time in half."

"I take it the two of you have already discussed this?"

"Yes, sir, and he's looking forward to it."

"Very well, then. If Knowles is onboard then you may proceed."

"Thank you, sir. Driskill, out."

A few moments later Lt. Ryan informed Commander Jackson he had just received the preliminary report from Houston concerning the engine problems experienced during launch. Jackson looked at Ryan and said, "Well, what's it say, Lieutenant?"

"To Commander, Pandora: Sirius and Houston agree the continuous gimbaling experienced during maiden launch was caused by over throttling the engines too early in the flight. Engineers believe the ship will perform as designed when standard launch protocols are followed. Telemetry since that time continues to indicate all systems on Pandora are nominal. Recommend using automated control system when executing powered maneuvers. Proceed with mission as planned. Houston, out."

Jackson was relieved but also slightly agitated by the report, and he sat waiting for some kind of comment about the ship's status from Starr. After a minute or so, it became obvious she was not going to make a statement of any kind. At that point he turned to Collins and declared, "Well, it's good to know there are no major problems with the ship, now that we're over..."

Starr broke her silence long enough to say, "1.1 million miles sir..."

"Yes... 1.1 million miles from home. A bit out of the way for a service call, don't you think?"

Starr's only response was, "Aye, sir."

"And how long for messages to reach us now, Captain?"

"Currently sir, it takes 59.3 seconds to receive a message from home."

Jackson boasted, "Mr. Collins, looks like we've learned something about the dependability of our ship... and our co-pilot has learned something, too." Collins looked at Starr but her eyes were on the forward monitor and she made no indication she had heard Jackson's statement.

Major Connor chose that moment to step back onto the bridge for the first time since Pandora launched. "Connor reporting, sir."

"Good to have you back, Major. Take your seat and prepare for resupply operations."

"Aye, sir. It's good to be back and if I may, Commander... I want to apologize to the crew for my actions during launch... and for what I said to Captain Starr."

Verna looked at him and answered, "No apology needed, Major. We all know you were drugged."

Connor hung his head and said, "Thank you, Captain."

Jackson paused a moment before adding, "Well there you go, Major. All is forgiven. Now, if you will, bring us alongside the supply ship and hold her steady while Driskill and Knowles do their jobs."

"Aye, sir. Rock steady it is. Stand by for deceleration. Ryan, prepare the crew for deceleration."

"Aye, sir. Attention all hands! Prepare for deceleration maneuver and report status."

Starr watched the green lights on her console come on one by one until all stations had reported. "All stations show green, sir. Supply ship now on long range visual, 25 miles and closing."

"Acknowledged," Connor said, "Firing RCS.... now!" Immediately the ship began to slow and over the next 30 minutes, Connor executed a series of RCS burns in order to match the supply ship's speed.

"Ryan, open a link to engineering and keep it open."

"Link available, sir."

"Commander to engineering. Commence resupply operations."

"Aye, sir. Opening Pandora fuel bay doors. Stand by to jettison spent fuel cells on my mark. Ready... mark! Cells 1, 2 and 3 away!" Driskill watched the empty cells float away from the ship then confirmed they were clear. "That's it, Commander. We're ready to receive. Sending command to supply ship to open her cargo doors."

As they closed in, Connor tapped the forward RCS one more time as the ships matched speed. "Nice, job Connor," Verna said. "We're traveling at 20,000 mph but the relative speed between ships is 0."

"Bridge, I'm opening access port 3 for Major Knowles and beginning MMU operations. Activating fuel cell crane now." For the next 40 minutes Knowles and Driskill worked as though they had done it all for many years and without a glitch between them. Driskill snapped three fresh fuel cells in place while Knowles made six round trips between the ships to bring aboard several large containers of food, water, and supplies as he finished just ahead of Driskill.

Major Driskill was about to store the crane when he glanced at his monitor to see Knowles spinning around like a top, then reversing direction before rapidly shooting straight up and over the ship. "Oh my god!!!" Driskill yelled. "Bridge! We've got a problem! I think the MMU has malfunctioned. As we were about to finish up, Major Knowles began spinning wildly, then he shot up over the ship toward the bridge! I can't see him anymore. Do you have him on your screen?" But as Driskill stopped talking he could hear what sounded like a female laughing. "What is that all about? Bridge, do you have him or not?"

"Everything is fine, Major. He's been giving us a little show out in front of the ship and now he's pretending to wash the windows. For some reason Starr thinks that it's funny. Jackson to Knowles."

"Knowles here."

"Major, if you've finished entertaining Captain Starr, would you mind getting your backside back in the ship?"

"Yes, sir. On the way." Knowles waved good bye and just as quickly as he had appeared, he was gone.

As Major Knowles returned to the airlock he could see a rather ominous looking engineer waiting for him, and once inside he got an ear full from Driskill. "Man, are you trying to kill me? I thought you were out of control and about to die and it would have been my fault, too. I'm the one that asked the commander to let you help."

"Sorry, Major. I apologize. I thought you knew I was just having a good time. I didn't mean to scare you. You do look a little pale, but hey, that thing is great! You've got to try it! You should see Starr use one of those things. How did we do on the time?"

"Pretty well. Right at half the time it would have taken me by myself, plus the time it took to get you back on board, but right now we're still 35 minutes ahead of schedule. I appreciate the help, but next time, tell me if you're literally going off on a tangent, ok?"

"Will do, and again, I'm really sorry I scared you." Driskill laughed and said, "Forget it. We're good."

"Jackson to engineering: If things are secure down there, we'd like to get back to the task at hand."

"Bridge, Driskill. Resupply is complete. We are ready to move and groove."

"Thank you, Major. Jackson out. XO, prepare the ship for max thrust."

"Aye, sir. This is the XO. All stations prepare for maximum thrust in 30 seconds."

"Ryan, send a message to Houston that we have completed resupply and are about to increase speed to 60,000 mph." Jackson asked, "Starr, why are you smiling like that?"

"Just looking forward to setting a new speed record for manned flight, sir."

"What is the record, Captain?"

"During its return from the moon on May 26, 1969, Apollo 10 set the record for the highest speed attained by a manned vehicle at 24,791 mph. We're about to make that look like they were crawling."

"Are we ready, Captain?"

"Yes, sir, Pandora is ready, willing, and able!"

"Mr. Connor, count it down."

"Aye, sir... 5... 4... 3... 2... 1." Connor hit the green button and said, "We have ignition. All five engines up and running at 20%."

At that point Starr began reporting ship condition and speed. "Confirmed! I'm showing 20% on all five engines. Thirty seconds until 60%. Speed rapidly increasing... 21,000...22,000... 23,000, throttle up to 60%. Good bye, Apollo 10!" Verna could feel a slight quiver in the ship as they exceeded 30,000 mph but it quickly faded. Then in just a few seconds Starr called out, "Maximum thrust... now!" All engines went to 104% as the crew found themselves plastered against their seats and near the point of passing out. Verna was having a hard time forming words but over the next few minutes she got the numbers out as best she could. "Engineering? Bridge. All systems... nominal...speed...36,000...rapidly increasing... 40,000... 45,000... 50,000... 55,000... MECO!"

Then as thrust ceased the crew began to recover. Verna looked around the bridge to see that several of the crew were close to passing out, including Ryan and Jackson. As soon as she could get up, she went to Ryan's console and called medical. "Are you there, Dr. Patel?"

"Yes... yes, I think so."

"We need you on the bridge, now! Several people have, or are close to, passing out."

"Acknowledged. I will be there shortly. Medical, out."

Verna went to Jackson and began to gently pat his face. "Commander, are you ok? Commander?" After a few seconds Jackson began to respond to her and tried to sit up in his seat. He seemed a little disoriented and his eyes were very red. "Commander, are you ok?"

"Yes, I think so. I have a pounding headache and my eyes hurt."

"I can see why, sir. I think a vessel in your left eye has burst, but the doctor is on his way."

"I'm fine, Captain. I just need to sit up a minute."

Finally, Dr. Patel arrived and began treating the crew. He first gave

Commander Jackson some bottled water and a couple of aspirin, and then moved on to the others. Once he could sit up and fully open his eyes, Jackson wanted a full status report from all sections, but for the moment all Starr could give him was that her board showed the ship on course, all systems nominal, and they were cruising at 60,102 mph.

Jackson looked at Starr and asked, "Did you pass out, Captain?"

"No, sir, not even close."

"That figures. I suppose you enjoyed it all."

"Well, yes, sir, but I'm sorry it was hard on you."

"I'll be fine, Captain. How's Connor?"

He's still out, probably because all of the drugs haven't completely cleared his system, but he seems to be breathing just fine."

As Connor began to regain consciousness, Starr handed him a bottle of water and some aspirin. Take these. They'll make you feel better."

"Thanks, Captain. What happened?"

"You passed out from the G-forces, but you're ok now."

"How long was I out?"

"About 2 minutes, sir, but you look ok to me."

"Commander."

"Yes, Mr. Ryan."

"Reports coming in now, sir. All stations manned and operational, sir."

"Thank you, Mr. Ryan. How are we doing, Doc?"

"Nothing to worry about, Commander. They will all be back to normal in a few minutes. It looks like the worst of it will be a headache or two. If the headaches persist, just take two aspirin and call me in the morning."

"Very funny, Doc."

"No, no, I'm not trying to be funny, Commander. I'm serious. That's about all you can do."

"Thanks for coming, Doc. If you're finished up here, how about make the rounds and check out the rest of the crew."

"On my way, sir."

"Commander?"

"What now, Ryan?"

"I just received a communication from Houston to stand by for a priority one message on emergency channel."

"Send it to my quarters, Mr. Ryan."

"Aye, sir."

Jackson stood up and said, "In my quarters, Mr. Collins. And Captain Starr, you come too. Mr. Connor, you have the bridge."

In a few moments Jackson pushed a button and said, "OK, Ryan, we're ready."

"Aye, sir. Still waiting."

"Commander, what do you think this is about?" Collins asked.

"I don't know. We're not scheduled to brief the crew for two more weeks."

"Ryan again, sir. Message coming in now." The monitor in Jackson's room lit up and there on the screen was the head of DSSF, General Peter Barrett.

Barrett began, "Greetings, Commander Jackson. I'm contacting you at this time to bring you up to date on an incident that happened yesterday just outside of Area 51. While on their way to DSSF HQ, the founder of Sirius, David Miller, and his top scientist, Rolf Stabroth, were caught on a security camera being abducted by the Greys just short of the base. NORAD was able to track the alien ship into space and Shepard currently has them on long range radar, but they will soon be out of our range. Oddly enough, it appears they are on a parallel course with Pandora and we believe they are headed for one of their bases on Mars. We know from past encounters that their ships are much faster than ours and if they maintain their current course and speed they will overtake you by 0200 tomorrow.

"Of course, we can't say with any certainty what their objectives are, or if the Greys even realize who they have taken or if the men are even still alive. Miller and Stabroth could have been targeted or it could just be a coincidence, but personally, I believe they knew exactly who they were getting and it's a move to curtail DSSF's progress with our new generation of spaceships. There have been some amazing breakthroughs recently that would almost put us on an equal footing with them, so you can see why losing either of these men would set us back several years."

"Within an hour of their abduction, the joint chiefs, DSSF, and the President met in an effort to develop a plan to deal with this situation. As you know, Commander, due to normal protocol, only the Commander in Chief can make a change to any DSSF mission that is underway and to that end the President will contact you shortly. Barrett out."

Jackson, Collins, and Starr all stood looking at each other like they had just seen a unicorn. "What do they think we can do about this?" Collins railed. "It's not like we can turn on a blue light and pull them over at the closest asteroid and ask to see in the trunk."

"I'm not going to speculate, Bill. Let's just wait and see what the President has in mind and go from there."

Then Collins looked at Captain Starr and asked, "Starr, what do you think?" But before she could answer Ryan was back on the comline.

"Commander, there's another message coming in. Would you like it there as well?"

"Yes, Mr. Ryan, send it through." Then there on the screen was the President.

"Good day, Commander. By now General Barrett has informed you of yesterday's incident. After meeting with all of the various entities involved with your current mission and taking into account the facts as we know them at this time, we have developed a plan to rescue the two men that were abducted. We all know the alternative, but let's put that on the back burner for today.

"Now, to the first matter at hand. As required by DSSF protocol, your mission change code is 'H.G. Wells.' Secondly, we have decided to retain your original mission but with a contingency for a rescue operation, should the opportunity present itself. There is much to cover before you reach Mars. In order to be ready, you will need to bring the crew up to speed now, as opposed to later. You are therefore authorized to share any and all information with the crew as you see fit. In one hour DSSF HQ will transmit the rescue plan. Meet with your crew ASAP.

"Lastly, you only have half of the puzzle, Commander. Captain Starr has the other half. As soon as this transmission has ended, take Captain Starr aside and give her this code phrase: 'Out of the mouths of babes.' After the two of you have talked you will have the entire picture. I know between the two of you the mission will be a success. Good luck Commander and God speed. This transmission ends now."

Without hesitation Jackson hit the com-link. "Mr. Ryan, encode and send the following on emergency channel: 'H.G. Wells, acknowledged.' Wait exactly 10 seconds then transmit: 'Orson Wells' and standby. There will be another message in one hour. Send it to us here."

"Aye, Commander."

"OK, Captain. You heard the President. Let's have it. Who are you, really?"

"You know who I really am, sir, but you don't know everything about our mission or about me. Last year I was selected by the President to head up a department within DSSF called Alien Eradication. The department's goal was to develop a multilayered, long term plan for dealing with every species of alien."

"Every species, Captain?"

"Yes, sir."

"How many species *are* there, Captain?"

"In order to keep everything in perspective and present a clear picture to you and the crew, I'd like to hold off on the specifics until after you have digested the next communication, sir. What I have to tell you will only make sense after you have been brought up to speed on your half of the story."

Jackson considered this for a moment and then acquiesced, "Very well, Captain. We'll wait."

Sitting quietly by, Collins looked bewildered by it all.

Verna asked, "What's the matter, Bill?"

"I guess I'm not sure I want to know the whole story. I think I liked life better when little green men were only science fiction."

"You mean little grey men."

"Fine! Little grey men. Does any of this seem surreal to either of you? I keep thinking it's all a bad dream and I'm going to wake up and be in bed with Mary and the kids."

Trying to make him feel better, Verna smiled and said, "If all goes well, Bill, you'll be back with them soon."

"I hope so. I feel bad not being there to protect them."

"But you are, sir. You're going to the source of the problem to protect them." Then she stood and stretched, saying, "How about I get us all some coffee while we wait?"

"Good idea," Jackson said. "Make mine black."

"Make mine half and half," Collins added.

"Half and half?"

"Yes, half coffee and half bourbon. Better yet, make both halves bourbon."

Verna shook her head a bit. "I'll be back in a few minutes."

Three cups later Ryan came over the com. "Message coming in now, Commander."

"Send it through, Mr. Ryan." For the next 90 minutes the group sat and listened to every bit of information DSSF had on the aliens and the rescue plan. When the message ended they spent another hour listening to Starr as she briefed them on Alien Eradication.

As they rejoined the bridge crew, Jackson told Fontaine to watch the aft radar for anything unusual and not long after, a small object appeared on his scope. "Sir, I have something. 900 miles aft, quickly closing on our high six."

"Configuration?"

"It appears to be a disk, sir, 40 feet in diameter and traveling at… no, that can't be right. Radar indicates it's moving at almost 90,000 mph. At that rate it will fly over us in…"

"One minute 52 seconds," Starr interjected.

"Starr is correct, sir. Less than 2 minutes."

Collins looked at Jackson and asked, "Should I sound general quarters, sir?"

"Negative. There's no time, but I don't think they're making a strafing run. Do we have it on visual?"

"Coming into range now, sir, but at their present speed we'll only have a visual for a few seconds."

"Put it on the screen and run cameras, Mr. Fontaine."

Suddenly the blurry image of a classic flying saucer became crystal clear as it flew directly over the Pandora and rapidly faded from view on the forward screen. "Did we get a decent snap shot of that ship?"

"I think the high speed camera got a few, sir, but they were moving very fast and the Hasselblad's weren't designed for this type of photography. Give me a minute to sift the photos. Their closest approach was 11.22 miles and they flew right over us!"

"Starr, what is their current course?"

"They are leading us straight to Mars, sir, but they will be there several days before us."

Collins turned to Jackson and asked, "Do you think they even saw us?"

"Absolutely," Jackson replied. "They were just saying 'Hello.'"

Collins, red in the face, launched into a rant, "That really pisses me off! The cocky little grunts! It's like they're leading us to their home. To think they can just zip by and thumb their noses at us like we can't do a thing about it really chaps my backside! Man!"

Jackson grinned at him a little then admitted, "Actually, Mr. Collins, to this point, we couldn't do much. They've been showing off like that for the last 40 years and we've hardly given them a reason to believe man would ever be a threat to them. But as someone once told me, don't ever underestimate your opponent. Isn't that right, Captain?"

"Aye, sir, dead on."

"In a few days we'll see if we can't give them a reason to show a little more respect for us, but for now the XO needs to advise the crew there will be a ship wide meeting at 0300. We've got a lot of work to do and the sooner we start, the sooner we'll be ready to go."

Chapter 10

At five minutes to the hour, the XO stepped over to Ryan's console and cleared his throat. "Now hear this. There will be a ship wide meeting at 0300. Secure your stations, activate monitors, and prepare to give your full attention to the commander. All stations acknowledge."

"Crew standing by, Commander."

"Thank you, Mr. Collins. Captain, come stand by me and face the main bridge camera as we explain what is to come. Mr. Ryan, is the crew ready?"

"Aye, sir. Whenever you are."

Commander Jackson looked straight into the camera and began. "Crew of the Pandora, what Captain Starr and I are about to share with you may come as a surprise to most, and while I think we all have suspected that extraterrestrials have been among us for quite some time, what you don't know is just how many there are and how extensive their domains have become. Since World War II, the world's governments have agreed to never openly acknowledge the existence of extraterrestrials. In fact, one of the goals for DSSF is to help keep all related information secure until such time as the government deems it necessary to share with the general population. That's part of why DSSF is a covert branch of service. What you are about to hear now is a little history and some important facts in an effort to help you understand why this mission is so important. It's my belief that we have a greater chance for success if we all have a clear understanding of what we are facing.

"For many centuries mankind has been terrorized by creatures from other worlds. They have abducted countless humans from all over the globe, perhaps even entire races. Many were never seen again. Those that returned were never the same. Our best scientists speculate that humans have been used for everything from medical experimentation to breeding stock, food, maybe even pets. But whatever the aliens' reasons have been, it's our mission now to bring an end to their reign of terror.

"A couple of hours ago, we were made aware that two of DSSF's most important scientists were abducted by aliens just outside of our home base in Nevada. In the last hour, that same spacecraft over flew the Pandora, apparently on its way to Mars, but before we get further into that I want Captain Starr to share what she knows pertaining to all of the alien life forms that we know of to date. Captain …"

"Thank you, Commander. While it's true we don't know nearly as much about the aliens as we would like, let me share what we do know. We have already confirmed that at least three different alien races have been visiting Earth for several thousand years and we are working to confirm the existence of two more. They range in size from two feet to just over ten feet in height. Their flight technology to this point has been vastly superior to ours but they are comparable to each other.

This leaves me to conclude that while they all seem to be independent species, they may have collaborated at some point in the past. The odds that three species would evolve at the same rate on different planets are astronomical, no pun intended. The closest alien base we know of is on Mars and we call them the Greys. The Greys have been the most common aliens reported in our lifetime. They were often seen during air battles of World War II and the pilots back then called them Foo Fighters. There are others that are not only larger, they may well be the most aggressive of the lot. I draw that conclusion because without exception, all of the abductees I have ever spoken with were returned by the Greys. I have never spoken to anyone that was returned by the other aliens.

"You may be wondering how we know anything at all about the aliens, but as limited as we are compared to them, the U.S. and our allies do have some intelligence gathering capabilities as well as direct contact with more than 60 living or dead aliens. Everyone has heard of the Roswell incident but there have been others, both in the U.S. and other nations. For example, only a few months after Roswell there was another crash in Hart Canyon near Aztec, New Mexico, that yielded three live Greys, many bodies, and a near intact spacecraft. Some of you may have heard of the now infamous Hanger 18 at Wright Patterson Air Force Base. In that incident it is believed they lost control of their spacecraft while investigating U.S. radar capabilities. We believe their proximity to a radar dome caused them to lose control and crash. In that instance, most of them were killed by the impact but not all, and that's why our Vindicators employ amplifiers on their radar. We intend to use high intensity radar as one of our weapons against them.

"Another crash happened when a Grey ship was following a pair of U.S. bombers over Suffolk, England. When it came too close to an F-111 Wild Weasel, the UFO crashed in Rendlesham Forest. So we know that intense radar or close proximity to even normal radar can disable their ships.

"Since the U.S. first began sending probes and landers to the moon and planets, we have seen many things and gathered a great deal of information about the aliens. From Pioneer, Ranger, and Surveyor, to Apollo, Mariner, Viking and Voyager, all of these probes and missions yielded much more than photos and soil samples. There was so much information gathered so quickly that it took a large group of scientists quite a while to sift through it all. Not to mention all that was learned from the dish at Arecibo. Scientists thought it might take decades to pick up anything that could be alien transmissions, but from the moment the dish went online there was a continuous flow coming from all directions. Some seemed to be coming from distant galaxies; others were located in our own solar system. In a nut shell, many of the rumors you may have heard are true. We know they have been observing our planet for at least three thousand years.

"The references to their involvement with multiple cultures throughout mankind's history, ancient drawings from around the world, the pyramids, the crystal skulls on multiple continents, Cydonia, The Face of Mars; the list goes on and on. Our top scientists now believe all of these things I've mentioned, all over the world and elsewhere, were made or built by aliens, or humans working with aliens.

"Did any of you ever wonder why the first astronauts to go to the moon were quarantined when they returned, even though they wore sealed space suits and were never directly exposed to the lunar surface, yet later missions spent no time in quarantine at all? When we first went to the moon in 1969, several Grey ships shadowed Apollo 11 and watched it from nearby. In addition to the rocks and soil samples Apollo 11 brought back from the moon, they also brought back an alien body from the crash site of Ranger 8, but the aliens observing the mission took no aggressive action toward the astronauts. Why the Greys never retrieved the bodies is anyone's guess. Whether they have no bonds to each other like humans do, or simply lack the technology to recover their 'brothers,' we don't know, but from Apollo 11's unofficial EVA, scientists concluded that one of the triangle ships was in the process of disabling the probe when something caused a collision that brought down both spacecraft, and still inside the wreckage several years later were five alien bodies. Due to the limited cargo space of the command module they were only able to bring back the smallest of the three and while they did all they could to hermetically seal the body in plastic, they were uncertain of the biological dangers from the alien body. As a precaution, the astronauts were forced into quarantine once they were back on Earth.

"Something else we know is that the Pentagon has had positive proof for at least four decades that extraterrestrials were visiting Earth and performing experiments on humans. Because their technology has always been vastly superior to ours, until now we have strictly been defensive, but with our recent advances and successes in near space, we are finally going on the offensive. Over the last 10 years the probes previously mentioned have been performing reconnaissance on many levels and in many places.

"My personal theory is that many eons past, three of the first five planets in our solar system were capable of supporting life: Earth, Mars and an unnamed fifth planet, but all that is left of planet number five is what we now call the asteroid belt. They were all approximately the same size, with a similar surface to present day Earth, all with large oceans, plains, mountains and vegetation that could support humanoid life forms. At some point, the inhabitants of the fifth planet successfully colonized Mars, but over time, like most colonies, it evolved toward independence and a struggle ensued for control of the planet. The struggle culminated in an interplanetary war, fought with weapons of great power. The Greys developed a weapon so powerful that it caused the breakup of the fifth planet, and all that was left is the asteroid belt we see today. But their victory was short lived.

"As the fifth planet exploded it took a large portion of the Martian atmosphere and magnetosphere with it. As a result, Mars rapidly lost most of its water and all of its vegetation as well. The Greys were quickly forced underground where they still live today, but these are not the same Greys that fought that war a million years ago. They are their descendants and bear little resemblance to their ancient ancestors. The few remaining structures that we refer to now as the Face, the Pyramid, the City, and Fortress are all that's left on the surface, and they are at least 20,000 years old. At one time they were all located on the equator, but the explosion shifted the planet's axis and rapidly changed the poles.

"Today, thanks to the Viking and Voyager probes and their ability to help us monitor and triangulate almost any point in the solar system, we now know the Greys have spread to several other locations, with well established outposts on Jupiter's moon Ganymede, Saturn's moons Titan and Mimas, and Neptune's moon Triton, but for now and for several reasons, we are focusing our efforts on Mars.

"We believe we now know where they live, approximately how many there are, their operational agenda, and how to stop them. As best we can tell, on Mars they live in one massive underground city and work for a common goal, in a manner similar to bees or ants. Our top intelligence resources have led us to believe their arrogance and under estimation of our abilities leave them vulnerable to attack, so here we are hurtling toward Mars at 60,000 mph, with 80 megatons strapped to Pandora. This concludes my portion of the briefing. Commander Jackson will take us the rest of the way."

"Thank you, Captain Starr, for your input and insight. So, where does that leave us with our mission? Currently there are several satellites orbiting Mars, Demos and Phobos. The Pentagon has been using them to study the Greys' movements for more than two years. From this we have identified three bases in close proximity. Once we arrive at Mars, a pair of Vindicators carrying four man crews will land at the opening to each base. Starr and DeArman will land their crews at Cydonia. Thomas and Lutz will land at the Pyramid, and Williams and Fuller will land at The City. Each team will make a quick attempt to rescue our scientists. But upon exiting these structures, whether they are rescued or not, the teams will seal the entrance to the bases with high explosives. Once all Vindicators are clear, Pandora will nuke them back to the Big Bang.

"HQ tells us the Greys use three different ships: saucer, cigar and triangle shaped. All of them have the ability to perform in any atmosphere. They are extremely fast, maneuverable, and most employ some kind of immobilizing beam that can be used against individuals or aircraft. We have never witnessed them using any thing that we would consider a conventional weapon. The Greys ships propel themselves by using some kind of magnetic field, and we know they have the ability to disrupt normal electronics at close range. To that end, our ships have been hardened to prevent electrical disruption, and we think our own EMP radar bursts will disrupt or disable their ships long enough to 'rip them a new one.' In addition to high intensity radar, all Vindicators have a 5-barrel 20mm electric rail gun that fires 2,000 depleted uranium rounds per minute. Pandora's guns use the larger of these type rounds and she carries a full complement of air to air and air to ground missiles.

"Initially, this mission only had one goal, but now we have two. The first and most important is to terminate the Grey's ability to raid Earth at will. The other is to rescue the two scientists that were abducted if at all possible. Either way, Pandora and her crew will do everything possible to eliminate the Greys as a threat. The scientists and this crew are considered expendable.

"Now, some of you may be wondering how we will be able to take on so many different tasks and for how long. Over the last four months several supply ships were launched ahead of Pandora. Those ships and the ones to follow will greatly extend Pandora's loiter capability. Hopefully, all will go well and we'll be returning to Earth in a timely manner, but if not, we will be well supplied and able to stay for as long as it takes. In one hour Major Knowles, his pilots, and support crew will begin practicing Vindicator launch, recovery, and live target practice. The rest of us will get some time in on the treadmills and attack simulators. I mean for us to be ready to strike at the earliest opportunity.

"Just before we get back to work, I have a question for anyone that would like to answer it. Can anyone besides Captain Starr tell me why this ship is named Pandora?" Jackson waited a good 30 seconds but no one could answer his question. Somewhat exasperated he said, "Starr, enlighten the crew."

"Certainly, Commander. According to mythology, Pandora was the very first woman created by Zeus, and he gave her to Epimethius to be his wife. As a wedding gift Zeus also gave them a beautiful small box that was labeled 'never open,' but over time Pandora naturally grew curious as to what might be inside the box. So she decided to open it just wide enough to take a peek inside, but as she cracked the lid the tiniest fraction thousands of horrible apparitions escaped into the world, and it was at that instant that Pandora unleashed every evil known to man."

"Precisely," Jackson confirmed, "and when we get to the Grey's house ... we're not going to just crack the box, we're going to fully open up on them with everything the Pandora has to offer. There's nothing like a good fire storm! This concludes this briefing. Everyone to stations. Dismissed!"

Jackson flipped off the main bridge camera, and then turned to Starr. "Thank you for your assistance, Captain."

"You're welcome, sir."

"What did you think of my Pandora analogy?"

"In keeping with the name of the ship, it was fine sir, but if I were going to use a woman to illustrate destruction, I would have gone with the 'Hell hath no fury...' bit."

Starr could tell Commander Jackson was slightly confused by her comment so she gave him an evil look and said, "The myth of Pandora can't hold a candle to a real woman's anger."

Her look and tone caused Jackson to literally take a step back as he replied, "Thanks. I'll try to remember that. But you know something, Starr, you actually scare me at times."

Then she smiled brightly and feigned innocence, "Little ol' me? I wouldn't hurt a fly, sir, unless he deserved it!"

Pretending to be caught off guard Jackson tried to shift her focus. "Well, look at the time. Isn't Major Knowles expecting you for 'touch and goes,' Captain?"

"Yes sir. On my way."

When she had gone, Jackson gave Collins a look that indicated he was a little concerned about Starr. Collins laughed but cautioned him saying, "There's nothing to worry about sir… as long as you don't make her mad."

Jackson nodded, "Add that to the list of things you're to remind me of."

"Not a problem, sir, but that list is getting longer by the day."

Unlike earlier moon missions on the Pandora, the ascent and descent stages were not always mated. When the Vindicators were flying patrol or cover for Pandora, the descent stage would be left behind in the launch bay and only attached when a surface landing was planned. Depending on where the Vindicator landed, the entire package would return. But there would be times that due to atmosphere or gravity, the descent stage would be left behind and used as a launch platform for the ascent stage as it was on Earth's Moon. The days passed quickly as the Vindicator pilots practiced dozens of touch and goes, initially with the ascent stage only. Along the way they found launching and landing a spacecraft without wheels in a small bay in a weightless environment was nothing like rolling a jet down a runway in the wide open spaces of an airport.

On day three of touch and goes the pilots quickly found that flying and landing only half of a Vindicator was much easier than the entire package. The landing pads on the descent stage of the Vindicators didn't slide very well on the decks of the bays, but after awhile Major Knowles and Starr taught them all how to use their RCS to lift themselves off the deck a few inches and then push the craft forward until they had cleared the bay opening. Once they were in space they could use their main engines to maneuver. The tricky part about landing was matching the Pandora's speed, and then tapping the Vindicator thrusters to get them down on the deck where the airmen could secure the vehicle. When the two stages were mated there were only a few feet of clearance and the tight fit didn't make things any easier.

By the last day of preparations the pilots had mastered launch and recovery as well as various attack formations. They had adapted to space flight much faster than Major Knowles had expected, and when he finally met with Commander Jackson in the ready room of launch bay 1 to assess the pilots' progress, Knowles told him he was very impressed with the entire squadron.

"Give it to me straight, Mike. Are they ready to be deployed in combat?"

"I believe they're as ready as they'll ever get, sir. I don't know what else we could do to prepare and besides, we're almost out of time. I think what they need now is some rest before the curtain goes up."

"What about your support personnel? How are they doing?"

"Actually, Commander, they may be the biggest surprise of all. Their turn around time on the Vindicators is nothing short of amazing. They can have a Vindicator refueled, rearmed, mated or separated in under five minutes and all while wearing a spacesuit and dragging their safety lines. These men are like watching a great pit crew at Talladega."

"Excellent, Major. You've done a tremendous job. Now I just need to check in with Major Driskill about the ship. Do me a favor and get him in here."

"Aye, sir."

In less than a minute Major Driskill appeared in the doorway with Knowles. "Driskill reporting, sir."

That was fast, Jackson thought.

"Major, I just wanted to check in with you to make sure Pandora is ready for combat."

"The ship is ready to go, sir. I've just completed a full inspection of all systems. The oxygen generators, RTG's, and engines are at 100%

and the Vindicators are fueled and fully armed. Of course, Captain Starr doesn't particularly like having her seat mounted on a pole so far off the floor, but the main platform beneath her chair gave us the hard points we needed to add extra seatbelts for her passengers."

"Everything sounds great, Major. You've done an excellent job as well. I suppose we're as prepared as possible. There's nothing to do now but perform the mission. If you will excuse me I'll get back to the bridge."

As Jackson stood to go, Starr came in and said, "Good evening, Commander. We're about to have a little get together in launch bay 2. Would you care for some coffee?"

"No, thank you, Captain. I need to get back up front. You and Major Knowles enjoy your evening." And with that, Jackson was gone.

Starr looked at Knowles and asked, "Does he look a little uptight to you, Mike?"

"I don't know. Sometimes it's hard to tell, but I would think he would be a little nervous, considering we're going to attack an entire planet in less than 24 hours."

"I suppose," she conceded. Turning her attention to a more immediate problem she asked, "Where's Blake with that pot?"

The urgency of her tone caused Knowles to laugh, "He's already out in the bay waiting on you."

"Then what are we waiting for? Let's go."

Arriving at the bay entrance they could hear music and people singing loudly, but their first glimpse of the group was Driskill and Collins standing by a large coffee pot plugged into a power inverter. Driskill looked up and announced, "Well, if it isn't the Coffee Maiden!"

"Where have y'all been?" Collins chimed in.

"We've been giving the Commander the low down on all of you."

Hiding the bottle of spirits behind his back, Collins asked, "Is he coming too?"

Verna giggled and tried to reassure him, "Relax Bill. He's on his way to the bridge. You're safe."

Scanning the bay, Verna noticed how many others had joined them. "Wow, guys! Did you invite the entire ship? I may not have enough coffee."

Driskill smiled and replied, "It's just a few pilots ... and Rangers ... and Marines ... and Airmen ... and us... so, yeah ... most of the ship."

"Oh well," she lamented, "it will go as far as it goes, I guess."

Collins was still standing with his bottle of dark brown fluid behind his back and looking nervous. Looking at them he argued, "I definitely don't have enough to share, so I'll just..."

"You'll just chip in like the rest of us," Driskill demanded. "Lutz brought all of his chips, Johns brought a huge sack of candy bars, and don't ask me where or how he got them but DeArman has about five dozen hot wings."

Verna looked amazed and excitedly asked, "Really? Hot wings? How?"

Driskill grinned and quickly answered, "Haven't you ever heard of 'don't ask, don't tell?' Just enjoy!"

Verna looked at Collins and said, "Now we know some of the other stuff that was smuggled aboard, don't we, sir?" Looking somewhat sad, he didn't answer. He just surrendered his bottle to Driskill and sat down.

The men all shared in the provisions and some even sang along with the music. A few even tried to dance a bit but the lack of gravity made it hard not to float around. Several of the men were talking about their girlfriends or wives or both, and how much they missed them. Looking at Starr, Boyd mentioned that it was nice to have a woman on board so they could remember what a female looked like. Being around a bunch of smelly guys all the time was enough to drive a person crazy. Harris agreed and said Starr looked a lot better than any of the other women he had seen in service. "Can you imagine a wife like that? I've been looking for a woman with brains to match her beauty all my life."

Lutz told them all to forget about Starr. He had heard that she was already committed. "Committed?" asked Tanner. "Committed to who? I don't see no boyfriend around here. I think I'll go talk to her right now."

Tanner walked over to Verna and asked if she would like to dance, but she politely declined saying, "I don't think it is possible to actually dance at the moment, Sergeant."

"Oh, come on," he said. "Looking like you do, in that tight leather suit, I bet you can really shake it up. Come on, give us a little show. It might be your last chance. We could all die tomorrow. What do you say?"

Now looking a little annoyed, she declined by saying, "Thank you again, Sergeant but I don't think so. And besides, I plan on making it back along with all of you."

Being turned down a second time made Tanner angry and he started toward her. "I said I want you to dance for me." But as he got the words out of his mouth, Captain Johns and the rest of the crew moved to stand between them. Tanner looked at Johns and said, "That's fine. She won't always have her own little army around. She'll dance for me. You'll see! You'll all see!"

Johns leaned into Tanner and quietly ordered him to return to his bunk and remain there until further notice. Tanner gave Verna a nasty look, then replied, "Yes, sir."

When Tanner was gone, Johns turned to her and tried to apologize, "I'm sorry, ma'am. I've never seen him act like that before. He's usually my best soldier."

Verna smiled and told him to forget it; no harm done. It was probably just being in space for the first time and the stress they were all under. "Don't hold it against him, Captain, because I won't."

"Thank you, ma'am, but if it happens again, I would appreciate it if you would let me know. I'd like to deal with it personally and not bother Commander Jackson."

Verna looked at him and said, "Don't worry, Captain. I'm not going to report him to the Commander, but if it's all the same to you, if there is a next time, I'll handle it myself."

Before Johns could answer her, Commander Jackson reappeared on deck and asked if he could join the party. "Certainly sir," Collins said, handing him a cup of coffee. Jackson said he didn't want to interrupt. He just wanted to make a quick toast, and then be on his way.

As they all held up their cups, Jackson said, "To a successful mission, the crew of the Pandora and all those who wait back home."

"To a successful mission and to those left behind," they all chimed in.

Starr saw a strange expression cover Jackson's face as he drank, then looking at Collins he asked, "Bill, where did you get this coffee?"

"From Starr, sir. Why?"

"Well, it has the faint flavor of ... whiskey."

Verna's eyes grew large as Jackson looked at her but before she could say anything Collins said, "Really sir? Maybe we need to wash the pot next time before we the make coffee."

"Wash the pot?" Jackson questioned. "Is that the best you can do?"

Collins looked at Verna and winked, then said, "That's my story and I'm sticking to it, sir."

"Very well, but just so you know, I expect my XO to be as sharp as a tack when we reach Mars."

"Yes sir, no problem sir, sharp as a tack, sir!"

Jackson looked as though he might say something more but then just smiled and said, "As you were."

As Jackson left, the Majors watched Verna slowly walk over to the aft door of the bay. "What's up with Starr?" Driskill asked Knowles.

"I'm not sure. Something about the toast seemed to change her appearance."

After Verna stood there a while looking out past the fairings at the small white dot called Earth, she placed her left hand flat against the acrylic glass door and said, "I love you. Come swiftly."

Driskill looked at Knowles and asked, "What did she say, Mike? I couldn't hear her. Did you."

"No, Blake, I didn't hear her either, but I didn't need to. She was talking to him."

"Him who?"

Major Knowles smiled then explained, "She calls him her soul mate."

After a moment, Driskill said, "I knew it! She's human after all… she has a heart of flesh. That could be her weakness in battle… or perhaps, her strength, but either way, we'll know soon."

The party was beginning to wind down when Collins spoke up and reminded them, "In less than nine hours we reach Mars. I think it's time that we all get some sleep. Crew dismissed!"

As they filed out of bay 2 and moved back to their quarters, Major Knowles emphatically told Verna to ignore Tanner. "He's just a blow hard. Don't let him bother you."

Verna smiled and said, "He didn't really bother me. I'm just a little surprised this hasn't happened before now. Commander Jackson was concerned about this type of thing when I was assigned to the ship."

Laughing, Driskill pointed out, "From the response Tanner got when he moved toward you, he's the one that should be concerned. I think it's obvious that you have a lot of friends on board and they seem to have your back."

"Yes, that was nice of them," she confessed, "but seriously, I can take care of myself. I'm not some damsel in distress."

"That's all well and good," Driskill agreed, "but friends are good to have, too. Don't you think?"

"Absolutely," she agreed. "Especially when they have the only portable coffee pot."

Knowles shook his head and mumbled, "You guys can stay up all night if you like. I need to get 40 winks. I'm out of here."

"Yeah, me too," Blake echoed. "I don't want to be asleep when it hits the fan tomorrow."

Verna told them both good night then went to change into her flight gear. When she was ready to go, she did her preflight then climbed into her Vindicator to clear her mind. From the mission, to the aliens, to those she loved, there were so many things racing through her mind that it seemed to be on fire, but then she remembered one of the first things her father taught her as a child and her mind began to settle down as she spoke out loud:

> "The Lord is my shepherd; I shall not want. He maketh me to lie down in green pastures. He leadeth me beside the still waters. He restoreth my soul. He leadeth me in the paths of righteousness for his name's sake. Yea, though I walk through the valley of the shadow of death, I will fear no evil. For thou art with me; thy rod and thy staff they comfort me. Thou preparest a table before me in the presence of mine enemies. Thou anointest my head with oil; my cup runneth over. Surely goodness and mercy shall follow me all the days of my life, and I will dwell in the house of the LORD forever."

Chapter 11

After she had finished praying and was convinced her Vindicator was ready to launch, Verna quietly made her way to the bridge. Arriving there, she found flight engineer Fontaine working at his station and alternate co-pilot, Captain Williams, sitting in her seat reading a novel about space travel. Walking over to him she glanced at the cover and said, "Really? <u>The Long Lost Space Man</u>? Should you be reading at your station, Captain? Aren't you supposed to be monitoring the helm and ship's systems?"

Looking up at her he answered, "It's a good book, and besides, the computer is doing all that. I'm technically just the baby sitter until we reach Retro. Unless something goes wrong, there's really not much for me to do."

Trying not to look too annoyed by his answer and resisting the urge to ask "who's babysitting the baby sitter," Verna began to slowly walk around the perimeter of the bridge examining each work station for any sign of a problem. Finding that all was well, eventually she made her way to the port window and stood for several minutes, just staring out at Mars. No longer a small reddish dot in the sky, the planet had grown considerably since they left home. Like the mission, it now loomed large and dead ahead.

At 0500 Commander Jackson arrived on the bridge with Connor, Collins, Ryan and the rest of day watch close behind. Looking at Verna he mumbled, "I'm not surprised." He asked her if she had gotten any sleep at all.

After a few seconds she replied, "I spent some time in prayer and quiet meditation, sir. I'm rested."

Jackson smiled at her then began barking orders. "Williams, you're relieved. Get to the launch bay and strap in. Starr, take your station. XO, notify the ship to stand by for retro."

In unison they all answered, "Aye!" and did as Jackson ordered.

As Williams left, Major Driskill came in and went to the vacant work station next to Ryan's. Quickly removing the temporary cover of what appeared to be an additional radar scope, he flipped a pair of switches then disappeared underneath the station. Ryan bent down and asked, "Whatcha doin', Major?"

"Let me know when the lights come on," Driskill replied. In a moment or two Ryan heard a beep and saw several L E D's flash on.

"Looks like you have power, Major." With that, Driskill stood up and began tweaking the controls until he had several nice sharp images on the screen.

Ryan looked at the screen a moment then questioned, "So it's finally online?"

"Yep, it's online," Driskill replied.

Commander Jackson turned to them and said, "I assume you two are talking about SRN?"

"Yes, sir. DSSF HQ activated it about two hours ago."

"Good. It couldn't have come at a better time."

"What is SRN?" Connor asked.

Jackson winced at the question then barked, "Starr, enlighten the Major, Captain."

"Aye, sir. SRN is the Space Radar Network. Over the last six years, an overlapping network of 55 radar satellites has been placed in proximity to every planet and their moons, except Pluto. While there is a time lag in some instances, depending on the location, the network will allow DSSF and its ships to monitor the entire solar system in real time. Now that it is fully operational we can see every space borne object from Neptune back to the Sun and anything in between. In short, we will know everything the aliens are doing in space and in some cases, on their respective grounds."

"Very good, Starr," Jackson said. Then he asked Ryan for an SRN status report.

"There's a lot of information here, sir. I mean, it sees everything. It will take me a few minutes to sort it all out but if I am reading this correctly the closest ship to us is our next supply ship, and it's already orbiting Mars. There is some activity around Saturn and Jupiter but it's all clear within 300,000 miles of our position. Except for our own satellites, we are the only thing in the area."

Jackson acknowledged Ryan's assessment with a nod then asked, "Connor, how long until Retro, Major? I hate burning off half our fuel to slow the ship."

"Fifteen minutes sir," Connor answered. Then he added, "There's no other way I can slow the ship sir. It takes a lot to get us moving and it takes a lot to slow us down."

Verna glanced at the commander and rolled her eyes. "What?" Jackson asked. Verna smiled and said, "Well, sir, actually there is a way to slow the ship and cut consumption by as much as 23% but it isn't a program."

Jackson looked at her and slowly stated, "No, no, no, Captain. This time we're going to follow the program exactly!"

"That's fine with me, sir. As long as we are able to achieve Trans-Mars-Injection, that's all that really matters."

Jackson looked at Collins to see him smirking and pretending not to be listening again. Jackson huffed then said, "Once again, Captain, I find myself knowing I'm going to hate the answer but I'll ask the question anyway. Just how can we cut deceleration fuel consumption by 23%?"

"That's easy, sir. We just manually flip the ship, or more accurately, we rotate the ship. The new shuttles will be doing it all the time. Pandora can do anything a shuttle can do." Jackson's head was spinning just thinking about it.

"Pandora is 425 feet long, Captain, and we're not a shuttle designed to perform that maneuver."

"That's correct, sir. But it's the same principle, just a larger ship."

Everyone was waiting for Jackson's decision, and as he looked at each man in the room, when he got to Connor, he said, "Well... you are the Command Pilot."

Instantly Connor began to complain. "Me? Rotate the ship? At 60,000 mph?" Just the thought of it terrified him, "Please, sir, don't ask me to do it. This time I readily defer to Starr. I don't want any part of it."

Jackson looked at Collins smirking at him, then asked Starr, "Are you sure, absolutely sure, you can 'rotate' the ship into the correct firing position?"

"Positively, sir. Remember? Lady? All it takes is a gentle touch, but there is one other thing.... we'll have to do it... twice."

At that, Jackson nearly came out of his skin as he exploded, "*Twice??*"

Without blinking she explained, "Well, yes sir, once to decelerate and then again to right the ship."

Jackson's blood pressure spiked and he broke out in a sweat as he stood there glaring at her. "Twice" he repeated to himself, as he considered executing the maneuver. Then he slowly sat down and began to buckle in and the others followed suit. "How long until retro, Captain?"

"Six minutes, sir." Then, except for the quiet beep of the radar station, the bridge fell silent as they waited for Jackson to make a final decision.

A long half minute followed as Jackson blankly stared at the forward view screen before he finally said to no one in particular, "One of us is crazy. XO, secure the ship for retro!"

"Aye, sir."

Collins stood by Ryan as he flipped the main switch on the comline. "Now hear this: All stations, secure for retro. Report!"

In less than 10 seconds, Collins calmly confirmed, "All stations report ready for retro, sir."

"Thank you, XO. Captain… rotate Pandora."

"Aye, sir!" Verna flipped off the autopilot and reached for her joy stick. Over the next 45 seconds she performed a series of RCS burns that slowly eased the ship around 180 degrees.

Back in the bays and engineering they were all totally amazed and a little confused, as they slowly realized that now their end of the ship was leading the way to Mars. Everyone that is, except for Major Knowles. He just smiled and said to himself, "She actually talked him into doing it!"

On the bridge, Verna looked up from her console and announced, "Pandora now in retro position. Standby to fire main engines at 10% in 3…2…1… ignition!" Right on cue the engines came up at 10%. The ship instantly began to slow but it had a bit to go before they would be down to 18,000 mph. Slowly she bumped the engines to 60% and held there as she once again called out their speed as they slowed toward Mars orbit. 55,000… then 50,000… all the way down to 18,000 mph. Except for Starr, during the entire procedure the crew was remarkably quiet. Now finally at the desired speed, she had one last maneuver to perform.

"Standby for secondary rotation in 3… 2… 1… now!" Again Starr slowly swung Pandora around until she had righted the ship. Arriving in the correct position she turned and smiled at Commander Jackson and said, "Pandora entering designated low Mars orbit of 60 miles, at 18,000 mph. Autopilot engaged."

Having achieved orbit, Jackson seemed to be very calm as he gave Starr a "well done," but his relaxed demeanor quickly changed as the SRN alarm went off. Ryan quickly scanned the screen and began reporting.

"Sir, radar shows 18, 19, no, make that 20 Greys' ships on a direct course for Pandora!"

Jackson looked at Collins and blared, "Well, I had wondered if they would even notice us but they aren't wasting anytime sending up the welcome wagon, now are they? XO, sound general quarters!"

"Aye sir!" Collins immediately hit 'Select all' on Ryan's console then boomed, "General quarters! General quarters! All hands, man your battle stations! This is not a drill!"

With the Klaxon blaring all over the ship, each man responded to their stations. Verna got out of her chair and made her way to the launch bays as rapidly as possible. Back in engineering, Driskill ran the output of both RTG's to 100% while Knowles and his crew prepared to launch the Vindicators.

Hurriedly Collins reported, "All gun ports showing manned; bay doors fully retracted; Vindicators standing by to launch."

"Acknowledged," Jackson replied. "Status of the saucers, Mr. Ryan?"

"Twenty Grey ships still heading straight for Pandora; 35 miles and closing rapidly."

"Mr. Ryan, get me CAG."

"You've got him, sir."

"Commander to CAG. Launch the Vindicators."

"Aye, sir. Launching now!"

Barely in her seat, Verna tapped her RCS and moved forward, flanked by DeArman and Shell. On the opposite side of the ship Lutz led Thomas and Faulkner out of the Bay and into space. After they had launched Captain Shell remarked, "I'd feel better about this if we were flying with the landing stage below us."

"Stop whining!" Starr snapped. "We're not going to be landing. You won't need it. Now cut the chatter!"

"Ok, gentlemen, remember how we practiced this. We know they're faster but not stronger. We want to bracket them one at a time and concentrate our resources until we gain some experience with these guys. Stay in double wingman formation, triangulate your EMP dishes on the same target, and encircle their ships with your fire. Short bursts only. Our rounds will travel a great distance out here, so be sure to keep your backs to the Pandora. We don't need any 'friendly fire' incidents. Only use your radar for 30 seconds or less at a time to prevent burn out. Now... let's light 'em up!"

Spread out like a bird's wing, two opposing lines moved toward a common point in space as six Vindicators aimed for the center of the Grey line. Lutz keyed his mike and said, "Rocket Babe, this is Falcon. We're on a collision course. What if they don't turn away?"

"Then there's going to be one heck of a mess when it's over," she replied.

Closing to guns' range, the outer five ships on either side of the Grey line broke off their formation and headed for the Pandora. The Vindicators, however, maintained their course toward the core of the saucer fleet and as they did, the Greys all began sending out oscillating EMP bursts of their own.

"Rocket Babe to Pandora. Looks like you have a dozen Grey ships headed your way."

"Roger, Rocket Babe. Commander says to send them on. We have some presents for our new friends."

Major DeArman joined the chatter to warn them, "Heavy D to Rocket Babe. I'm picking up a huge EMP spike that's causing my systems to blink on and off but I still have intermittent control. Nothing knocked out yet."

"I see it," Starr answered. "Try to stay on course. We're closing in on firing range. Standby to activate your EMP radar on the center three ships in 3... 2... 1... now!"

As they all focused their EMP dishes toward the center of the Greys' line, they could see all three of them begin to wobble slightly. When Starr saw that, she radioed, "EMP radar seems to be working. Bring the heat!" At that point all six Vindicators opened up on the Grey ships directly in front of them. In just a few seconds a dense wall of lead began shredding the saucers and sending pieces of their ships in all directions. Starr closed in on the closest wobbling ship and used her cannon to bore a hole right through the center of it. After a few seconds the saucer suddenly began to spin very fast just before it exploded, sending out debris in all directions.

"Yeah!" yelled Heavy D. "That's what I'm talking about! Nothing like a little depleted uranium to get a party started. That's a lot of trash for a little ship!"

"Glad to see it," Starr said. "But there's no time for celebrating. Let's get back to work!" As the words came out of her mouth, Lutz and Thomas both took out the ship in front of them but this time there was no explosion, just a pair of saucers tumbling and arcing back toward the planet.

Then, off to their far left, DeArman took out another saucer with only cannon fire.

"Nice shot, Heavy D! Now let's get after the rest." The Vindicator pilots were gaining experience and confidence quickly, but Starr wouldn't let them get cocky.

"We're doing great but let's stick to the game plan, no freelancing! We're through the first wave, that's all. There are 16 more to go, so let's get to it. On my mark, everyone break left and head back toward Pandora. Mark!"

Back on the bridge, Commander Jackson asked Ryan for a status report on the Vindicators. "Vindicators have eliminated four Grey saucers and have suffered little damage thus far. At the moment they are 32 miles out but are inbound to Pandora. Ship's gunners took out five more, sir."

"Excellent!" Jackson said. "Maintain firing!"

On their way back to defend the Pandora, the pilots could see the remaining saucers flying very fast and forming a wide circle around the ship. "What the heck are they doing, Falcon?" asked Shell.

"I'm not sure, Black Jack. Maybe they just like flying in circles."

Starr broke in and warned, "I believe they intend to surround the ship and…" Just then, the entire fleet of Grey ships sent out one massive EMP that took down the Pandora's RTG's and caused a complete power failure. As the pulse reached the Vindicators, Starr heard several pops as sparks shot from below her seat. Less than a second later, she and the entire squadron completely lost power as they were left floating dead in space.

The Pandora back up generator kicked in quickly, but it was limited compared to the power provided by the RTG's. Unfortunately for the pilots, the Vindicators had no such back up and were left drifting. The emergency lights kept the bridge from being completely dark, but for the most part the Pandora had been disabled.

"Fontaine, report!" snapped Jackson.

"Main power is out, sir. Emergency generator is coming online now. How shall I direct power?"

"Allocate power to the guns. Ryan, get Driskill on the line."

"Aye, sir."

"Driskill here."

"Major, it seems we have a slight power problem."

"Working on it, sir. It's going to take a minute or two to assess."

"You've got 30 seconds. I need main power back now!"

"Aye, sir. Standby."

On the bridge they could see the Grey ships swarming the Pandora, but were unable to do much about it at the moment.

"Time's up. What about it, Driskill?"

"I have some good news and some bad news, sir."

"Let's have the good news first, Major," Jackson demanded.

"Sir, the good news is that overall our electrical systems are ok, except for a few minor problems that I can repair.

"And the bad news?"

"They tripped every breaker on the ship. It's going to take some time to get it all back online again. Oh, and there's one very bad thing sir."

"What's that, Major?"

"The little snots fried my coffee pot, sir. It's a goner."

"That doesn't sound so bad, Major. I think you can make it without coffee for a while."

"Well, it's not me, sir. It's Starr. She's going to be very upset. Who's going to tell her?"

Seeming a bit confused, Jackson looked to Collins for help but all he said was, "Don't look at me, sir. That kind of thing is above my pay grade."

Grinning just a bit, Jackson replied, "Just get main power back online, Major. I'll handle Starr."

"Aye, sir. Driskill, out."

In another minute or so main power was restored to the bridge. "That's better," Jackson said. "Mr. Ryan, how many saucers are we dealing with now?"

"We have ten surrounding the ship and one has landed on the deck of landing bay two."

"What?!" Jackson yelled. "Get me Captain Johns right now."

It took a few seconds but finally someone answered on the landing bay intercom. "Knowles here. What's going on down there, Major?"

"At the moment sir, we're kind of busy. Captain Johns and Ranger Baker have two of the little Greys guys pinned down in the ready room. No…wait, they're making a run for it!"

The bridge could hear several shots as gun fire erupted in the bay. In a few seconds, Knowles came back and said, "They got them, sir! Both of the aliens are dead and their ship has just flown out of the bay. What should we do with the bodies?"

Jackson thought a moment before growling, "Have one of your men sweep them out into space and clean up the blood or whatever."

"Well, that's the thing, Commander. There are holes all the way through them, but they didn't bleed at all."

"Good." Jackson said. "Less to clean up. Jackson, out."

"Mr. Ryan, how close are the Grey ships now?"

"Approximately 2 miles, sir."

"Has that been their distance the entire time?"

"Except for the ship that landed in bay two, they've pretty much maintained that distance the entire time."

"I see. Get Driskill back."

"Driskill here."

"Major, it's time we made a little EMP burst of our own and I want to use both RTG's at max power when we do."

"Oh, I don't know sir. It's only designed to handle one RTG. Using that much power would be very risky. We could end up damaging our own ship's electronics or at least the emitter, and that I can't repair. Not to mention the Vindicators. They're out there somewhere and have no idea what we're planning to do."

"I'm willing to take the chance, Major. How soon can we do it?"

"Give me a few minutes, sir."

"Let me know as soon as you're ready, Major."

"Aye, sir."

Back in engineering, Major Driskill was talking to himself and working feverishly to route all power to the main emitter. "I don't like this at all. That's going to be a lot of power running through one emitter and if it blows... well, let's not think about that. Ok, that's got it. We're ready to go... Driskill to bridge."

"Jackson here."

"It's ready, sir. Put your fingers in your ears and press the button whenever you're ready, but if it blows every system on the ship, I've gone fishing!"

"Acknowledged, Major."

"Mr. Ryan... ship wide, if you will."

"Go ahead, sir."

Jackson leaned forward in his seat and said, "All hands, standby. We are about to use all the power we can muster for an EMP burst in 3... 2... 1... Now!"

Fontaine hit the EMP switch on his console, unleashing a massive power flow to the main emitter.

In less than a second, the Pandora suffered a 96% reduction in power, as systems all over the ship went down. Electrical shorts caused several small fires and as smoke filled the bridge cabin, Ryan lost radar and the main viewers. He and the other officers weren't able to see that every saucer around them had begun to wobble and then slowly tumble away from the Pandora, much like the Vindicators had done when they were hit by the Grey's pulse. Jackson yelled, "Ryan, alert the damage control crews and get the viewers back on, now! We need to see what's happening."

"Working on it, sir."

It took several minutes to extinguish all of the fires but as the smoke began to clear, Collins went to the starboard window of the bridge and looked out. There he saw several of the saucers slowly drifting away. With a tone of great satisfaction he said, "We did it! Looks like we got 'em, Commander. They couldn't handle it! Fly over us... that'll show 'em! And they sure look dead in the water to me."

Jackson went to the port window to check the other side and saw the same thing: five or six Grey ships floating sideways or slowly tumbling away from the Pandora. After a moment he said, "I don't trust them, Ryan. Tell the gun crews to make sure they nail them all for good measure and get me a status report on the fighters."

"It's going to be a few minutes, sir. The pulse took out our radar and the main communication dish but engineering is already on it."

"Understood. Get me something as quickly as you can, Mr. Ryan."

As the gun crews mopped up, a single saucer managed to regain enough power to break away. One of the aft gunners saw it but before he could respond, it had escaped.

Meanwhile, the Vindicators were drifting apart and slowly tumbling in the general direction of the Pandora.

"Starr to Lutz... Starr to DeArman... Starr to anyone... Ok, this is not good and it's getting cold in here fast. Everything looks to be in working order. It just isn't working." Verna unbuckled herself and proceeded to remove the cover from the electrical panel beneath her seat. Finding the main breaker, she hit reset and suddenly power was back up. Talking to herself she said, "Oh, it can't be that simple… can it?" Climbing back into her seat she regained control of her ship and tried again to contact the others. "Rocket Babe to Heavy D… anyone?" There was no response. "Ok, we'll have to do this the hard way."

Verna looked at her radar screen to find it totally dark. Not good, she thought. Let's try visual. Looking out of the small window of her craft, she caught a glimpse of something white about a mile away. In no time Starr was next to the tumbling Vindicator but she couldn't see anyone inside. Then seeing the pilot's name on the ship she said, "It's DeArman. Good. I guess I'll have to improvise a little here." Then Starr began to roll her ship at the same rate as the powerless Vindicator, so she could maintain line of sight with his windows. She flashed her tracking lights a few times and before long she saw him looking out of his port window. Using old fashion Morse code, she flashed how to reset his system and in a couple of minutes Heavy D was powered up and ready to go.

"We have to let the others know how to get back up and running."

"That would be fine," he said, "except my radar is out, remember?"

"That's not a problem. They can't have drifted very far. I can locate them based on our position when we lost power and the rate of drift, then we'll do what I just did with you."

"That's fine by me," DeArman responded. "Let's go!" One by one Starr found the other pilots and they were all able to regain main power except for Faulkner.

After some consideration Lutz asked Starr, "What do we do now, Captain? If Brick's ship can't power up, how do we get him home?"

"Well, it appears that he's going to have to come to one of us."

"What? He's going to have to leave his ship and come to one of us?"

Lutz repeated in amazement. "And how does he do that? None of us have a tether?"

"I realize that," Starr replied, "but he only has three options. He can eventually freeze, suffocate, or try to make it aboard one of our ships."

Again, 'Doubting Lutz' asked, "What is he supposed to do, jump to one of us and then hold on all the way back to the ship?"

"Hardly," Starr groaned. "This will be easy! We'll just go overhead hatch to overhead hatch. All I have to do is move under his ship and all he has to do is turn his ship upside down and drop into mine."

"What about the EMP dishes on top? Won't they act like a standoff, or worse, break off?"

"No problem," she said. I'll just rotate my ship until we're back to back and then get close enough for him to grab the top of my hatch and pull himself through."

Lutz came back with, "I don't know. Sounds crazy to me but since it's Brick's life, I guess it's his call."

"Yes, it is," she said. Then Starr flashed her suggestion to Faulkner.

After a few moments to think it over, he flashed back, "Roger."

As the other pilots held their collective breath, they depressurized their ships and opened the top hatches. Starr moved her ship beneath his and as the space between them closed, she reversed the forward side of her ship in relation to his, and moved up as close as she could to his fighter. Once her fighter was within three feet of his, she aligned the hatches of each ship perfectly and motioned for him to get on with it. Although Faulkner was scared half to death and working upside down, he managed to climb to the opening and stick his head out. Then, looking down at Starr, he reached for the rim of her hatch just as his ship began to float away from hers, but he was safe. She had anticipated the movement and was compensating for the drift. Faulkner reached out again and this time he managed to grab the VHF antenna next to Starr's hatch. He used it to pull himself to her ship, and once he was completely inside, he quickly sealed the hatch.

"Fantastic!" yelled Lutz. "That was amazing! Now all we have to do is find the Pandora."

"I've got her on radar at 356 miles and pulling away," Starr reported, "but something isn't right… Bullet, what are you seeing on your scope?"

Major Thomas checked his radar then replied, "I'm not sure… what I'm seeing. I assume the big thing is the Pandora, but it looks like there's a lot of… what could be pieces of the ship, trailing along with her."

Starr looked at her scope again and confirmed, "Yeah, that's what I was wondering about, too. They're not responding to my calls. Let's just hope we have a ship to land on when we get there, and at the moment she's pulling away from us. We're going to have to punch it if we're going to catch her. Form up on me and let's go!"

As they began to catch up to the Pandora, the debris field trailing her became denser, and the closer they got, the heavier it became. "Man, it must have been one heck of a fire fight," DeArman said. "Rocket Babe, how much of this junk is from the Pandora?"

"Well, from what I've seen so far, I'd say very little. I haven't seen anything that remotely looks to be from Pandora but it is getting a little heavy. Let's drop a few miles below the flow, before we fly into something we can't see."

After a minute or so Black Jack asked her, "So you think the Pandora is ok?"

"I do," she responded. "The return from Pandora on my radar is getting bigger and there's nothing within five miles of it. I think the pulses may have taken out their comline but either way, we'll know for sure in a few minutes."

Now only five miles out, the debris was beginning to trickle down to nothing and the pilots could clearly see an intact Pandora. As they began their final approach, Starr tried to contact the ship again but got no response. "I'm not seeing any running lights, and I want to know they see us before we try to land," she said. "101st, hold this position while Brick and I do a quick flyby of the bridge."

As the others waited, Starr flew directly in front of the Pandora then turned her ship around to face the bridge as she flew backwards ahead of them. "Is that who I think it is?" asked Jackson.

"What do you think?" answered Collins, as he walked over and stood right in the port window. Seeing him, Starr flashed her lights and asked for permission to land.

"What's she doing?" Jackson asked.

"Morse code, sir. She wants to know if the 101st Vindicator Wing has permission to land."

"Just give her a thumbs up and notify CAG his kids are home." Seeing Collins just standing there with a strange look on his face, Jackson asked him what he was doing.

"Well, sir, it looks like Starr picked up a passenger."

"A what?!" Jackson questioned, as he came back to look for himself. Looking at Starr's fighter he saw two people waving at him, one from each window. Jackson looked at Collins and said, "We need to get to the landing bay, fast! Let's go Mr. Collins."

Seeing Collins wave her in, she returned to the squadron to lead them back to the ship. "Ok, gentlemen, we've been invited aboard, but once we're on deck I want everyone to report to the ready room for debriefing."

"Acknowledged," replied each pilot.

Major Knowles stood in the landing bay control room and watched his squadron land one by one counting them as they came aboard. When it became obvious that one was missing he grew very concerned. As soon as the doors were closed and the bay pressurized, Knowles ran to Starr's fighter to ask what had happened to Faulkner.

"Faulkner? Faulkner? Oh yes, I do seem to recall a Faulkner."

"Well, what happened to him, Captain? Where is he?"

"Oh... he's right behind me, sir."

Just then, Major Knowles looked up to see Captain Faulkner coming through the forward hatch. Trying not to look too concerned he said, "So he's ok?"

"Yes, sir, he's fine, I think... He hasn't removed his helmet yet."

Knowles made a sour face and shook his head. "Let's don't go there." Then after a minute he yelled, "Where's the top half of my other Vindicator, Captain?"

"Well, that's another story Major. It's... not coming back."

When everyone had assembled for the debriefing, the pilots listened as Commander Jackson explained their tactical situation. When he was finished Starr related the pilots experience and efforts against the Greys. Before concluding, Jackson asked Major Driskill for a complete run down on the ship's current fighting status.

"Sir, repairs are being made throughout the ship and we have restored power levels to 65%. All damage from our encounter with the Greys appears to be internal. There is no evidence of external damage to the ship, probably because none of them exploded. All weapons systems are fully operational but radar will not be restored for another 6 to 8 hours. The upper stage of Vindicator #3 was lost in battle, leaving us with an extra landing stage. Vindicator #2 is currently without radar; the other four are fully operational. All five are being refueled and rearmed as we speak, and except for the radar on #2, they will all be ready to go again within the hour. Lastly, the resupply ship is now orbiting the planet and seems to be intact, but until we get to it I can't say for sure."

Jackson stood and thanked Driskill for all of his hard work and the report, and then he laid out his intentions for the rest of the mission.

"Our original itinerary called for us to resupply the ship as soon as we reached Mars, but our immediate encounter with the locals and the kidnapping of the scientists has put us off script just a bit. Add to those two factors that one of the Grey ships managed to return to their base, and it's my belief that our best course of action is to go ahead with the rescue / assault, ASAP. I do not want to risk another confrontation while we are less than 100% or in the middle of a resupply operation. I have therefore decided that we will proceed with the mission as soon as the Vindicators are ready to go. XO, notify the Marines and Rangers to prep and standby."

Turning to Driskill and Knowles he asked, "How long before your men can have the Vindicators mated with their landing stages and ready to go?"

The Majors conferred and Knowles finally said, "Less than an hour, sir."

Jackson nodded his approval, "Then let's move it! Operation *Dust Storm* will begin in one hour!"

Chapter 12

January 27, 1982, 0600 hours.

Commander Jackson walked onto the bridge to find the crew already fastened in their seats. Looking at Collins he asked, "XO, are we ready?"

"Aye, sir. Crew is standing by."

"Very well. Mr. Connor, put us in attack position."

"Aye sir; firing RCS now." Connor performed several burns to change the Pandora's speed and altitude, and in just a few minutes he announced, "New orbit achieved. Now orbiting at 110 miles and 8,000 mph."

"Very well, Major. Mr. Ryan…ship wide."

"Aye, ship wide, sir."

"This is the Commander. I just want to remind all of you what is at stake here. We are about to put an end to hundreds of years of terror, abductions, and God only knows what else. This mission has three goals: get down, get the hostages and get back. Our success depends on everyone staying on schedule and doing their job. The engineering crew is working feverishly to restore radar but until we can see the Vindicators, the pilots will be responsible for all flying protocols, and because Pandora is now in a decaying orbit, there is no room for error or delay. We cannot maintain our course more than three passes before we have to achieve a higher orbit or spiral in. We must fire our nukes by the third pass, and regardless of where the landing parties are, we will fire those nukes. God speed to all!"

Jackson told Ryan to transmit his logs to HQ and provide real time links to DSSF tactical. Then he swiveled around to Collins and barked, "XO, sound general quarters!"

"Aye, sir! General quarters! General quarters! All hands, man your battle stations!"

In the control room, Knowles watched the last of the marines and rangers board the fighters, then he raised the launch bay doors before picking up his com link. "Strike Leader, this is CAG. You are cleared for launch."

Pressing the button on the side of her helmet, Starr answered, "Strike Leader to CAG: acknowledged." Then looking at Captain Johns she asked, "Are you, Brown and Fisk, secured?"

"We're all good," Johns assured her. "Just get us to the door. We'll take it from there."

"No problem, sir. Here we go!"

Starr tapped her RSC and moved out of the bay as the others followed suit. Once they were clear of the ship, she fired her engine for just a second to start their descent. As the Pandora arced away from them, she quipped, "Our next stop is Cydonia, Captain. Just relax and enjoy the ride. Heavy D stay close to me and when you land try to keep a distance of at least 200 feet. We don't need to be kicking up rocks at each other."

"I'm aware," Johns said. For about 15 minutes, five Vindicators fell toward their targets. Then at 50,000 feet they all fired up engines again to begin slowing for landing. "How long?" he asked.

"About five minutes, sir, and you'll be the first marine on Mars. How do you like that? You can't really be the first man since the hostages are already there, but first marine is good too, right?"

Johns smiled and replied, "I love the way you always think of these kinds of things, Captain. You must keep your boyfriend well entertained."

Giggling Verna answered "Oh, I do, and he keeps me entertained as well," she added with a wink. Refocusing on her landing site, Starr said, "Thirty seconds to touchdown. Stand by." Through her windows she could see Heavy D close by, Lutz and Thomas closing in on the Pyramid, and Shell and his crew about to land at The City. When they were all down Starr called out, "Strike Leader to all pilots: clock starts now. You have 25 minutes to make your sweep and set charges. When you have completed your tasks get back to your ships ASAP and stand-by for liftoff. Go!"

As soon as they were depressurized they were out the door and down the ladder. Johns took point as they made their way to what looked like an opening. Arriving at their target, he noted, "Man! That is one small door, Captain. It's going to be a tight squeeze."

"I can make it larger," Brown said with a smile.

"I'm sure you can, son, but let's see if we can get in without waking the neighbors, ok? Brown, you stay here. Set the charges and wait for us. You'll be our radio man and relay for us. I'm pretty sure we won't get a signal once we're inside."

"Yes, sir."

One by one the others pushed through the tight opening and into complete darkness. Turning on their helmet lights they could see they were in what appeared to be an endless tunnel. Fisk reached into his supply pouch and took out a small bag of very fine white sand. Taking a handful of it he tossed it up to see if there were any currents in the tunnel. As they watched the sand float quickly toward the opening where Brown was waiting, they all smiled.

"Ok, let's keep moving," Johns whispered. "If there's a draft, there's got to be something up ahead."

It wasn't long before Brown saw some of the sand float out of the tunnel opening. "Brown to Johns: did you find anything, over?"

"Not yet. I'll let you know if we do."

"Roger, sir, Brown out."

Continuing on about another hundred yards they came to a branch in the tunnel and they could see light at either end. "What the heck?" Johns... "Now what?"

DeArman spoke up and suggested, "We have to split up. I'll take my guys and go right. Y'all can go left."

"Good call," Johns agreed. "We'll meet back here in 10 minutes. Go!"

At the Pyramid, Lutz, Thomas and their crews had found a giant open structure but it appeared it had been abandoned a very long time ago. There were some strange markings that almost looked like Egyptian hieroglyphics, and at one point they saw a drawing that looked like some kind of giant beast with four arms. "I wonder what that thing represents," Thomas said.

"I don't want to know," replied Lutz. "Let's get some photos, complete the sweep and get out of here. I don't see anything to indicate anyone has been here since the world was formed." Hurrying along, they were back outside setting their charges.

Landing at The City, Captain Shell and his men found what appeared to be an ancient gate that led them into an underground bunker. Light was coming from somewhere but the source was not obvious. It was almost like the walls were glowing. Some form of writing covered every wall and as they crept deeper into a large open corridor, they suddenly felt the ground begin to shake. Something large was coming toward them. Shell looked at Dietl and asked, "Alright, Marine. What do we do?"

"The clock is ticking. We investigate. Quickly!"

Deeper into the bunker they crept until they rounded a corner where they came face to face with the largest, nastiest looking creature they had ever seen. Twice the size of a full grown elephant and covered with scales, all four of its huge yellow eyes locked on them. Then six cat-like legs, with claws sharp as an eagles and more than three feet long brought it nearly to them in only a few leaps. "My God! What is that?" Specialist Harris asked, his voice shaking.

"Unholy moly!" grunted Boyd. "I got to get me some of that!"

"Fire!" screamed Dietl, as the gigantic beast charged them. All four men opened up on it with everything they had, but with little to no effect.

"What the devil?" yelled Shell in disbelief. "We're not even slowing it down."

Boyd pulled a grenade from his suit and lobbed it at the head of the creature. The explosion left the "thing" temporarily stunned but only for a few seconds.

"Get to the ship! Get to the ship!" yelled Captain Shell. All four men began to move as fast as they could but it was a long way back. They cleared the bunker and were about halfway to the Vindicator when the wounded animal recovered and began to pursue. Now out of the bunker, they found the surface covered in small rocks and sand, making it harder to move quickly without falling down. If a suit ripped, it would be all over.

With the creature rapidly closing on them, Shell was the first one to reach the ship and went up the ladder as fast as he could. Dietl followed him in as Harris paused on the egress platform to cover Boyd. Unfortunately, he found that his gun was completely ineffective against the scales of the animal and two of its massive paws grabbed Boyd, snatching him from the ladder. Harris emptied his gun on its head but the monster paid no attention to him. Bullets ricocheted in all directions as the creature shook Boyd violently then held him high in the air over its mouth. Just as it was about to swallow Boyd whole, he managed to yank another grenade from his suit and pulled the pin as he disappeared into the thing's throat.

"My God! It ate him alive!" Harris screamed. Two seconds later the grenade exploded, blowing a large hole through the side of its neck. When the animal fell it hit the ground hard enough to rattle the Vindicator.

The three men were stunned by what had just taken place, but after a moment or two, Shell snapped them out of it with, "Get strapped in. We're leaving."

"No, Captain, it's not time," Harris called out. But then he saw the creature begin to stir and quickly changed his mind. "Did that thing move?"

Shell nodded his head, "I think so."

Harris looked at him and quickly conceded, "Never mind about the time. Good call. Let's go, now!"

No one had to ask Shell twice and he set the controls for liftoff. "Going in 3… 2… 1… Now!" Shell pushed the button and the retention bolts blew beneath them as the engine ignited. In a literal flash, they were lifting off just as the creature managed to get to its feet and jump straight up after them, missing the ship by mere inches.

"That was close!" yelled Dietl. "Another second and we would have been scrap metal!"

"I'm going to have the last word on this subject," snarled Shell, as he angled back toward the lander. Realizing how close they came to being the second course at dinner, Dietl couldn't believe the ship was making a sharp turn back.

"What are you doing, sir? Let it go!"

"No way! That thing killed Boyd and now I'm going to kill it!" As Shell completed his circle he saw the living nightmare making its way back to the gate. Turning inbound, Shell reached for the grip on his gun and just as the creature centered in the cross hairs, he squeezed the trigger. Firing 100 rounds per second, Shell ripped his target to shreds, blasting great chunks of flesh all over the area. Then as he watched the creature disintegrating under his fire, he leaned hard on the stick to bring the fighter to the proper attitude for lifting into space and accelerated upward at full throttle.

"Nice shooting, Captain," shouted Harris. I'm glad you got him."

"Me, too," answered Shell with a deep sigh of relief. "Me, too."

As the two men celebrated their revenge on the creature, Dietl waited a few seconds before saying, "I guess now wouldn't be a good time to mention this but… we forgot to set the charges."

"We forgot what?" yelled Shell.

Harris grinned and asked if they wanted to go back. Dietl just shook his head and said, "No!"

Once he had collected himself, Shell radioed the Pandora and the other teams listened in as he told them what had happened. When he had finished his report, Collins answered, "This is the XO. Glad the rest of you made it out. We'll make the course adjustments to pick you up but it will have to be after we collect the others."

"Roger that, sir. We'll be happy to wait."

Soon after, Lutz and Thomas reported in to say their teams had completed their sweeps and set their explosives but they had not seen any signs of life, scientists or otherwise. "We're standing by for liftoff to rendezvous."

"Roger ready," replied Ryan. "Hold for Starr's team."

Collins looked at Jackson and said, "It's not looking good for the scientists, sir. I was really hoping we could save them."

Jackson seemed to be in deep thought as he told Ryan to get Starr's group on the line. "Aye, sir. Specialist Brown is standing by."

"Brown, this is Commander Jackson. Give me a status report."

"Well sir, it's been pretty quiet since they went in. I thought they'd be back by now. We're running out of time."

Then Brown heard something over his walkie-talkie. He thought he heard Johns say, "There's one on the left!"

"There's another on the right…we can't get them all. Keep firing! Keep running!" shouted Starr.

The signal was getting stronger, and looking down the tunnel Brown could see flashes of gun fire and helmet lights bobbing up and down. "Pandora, this is Brown. They're coming but I think there's some kind of fire fight going on. Wait. Now I can see several people coming this way and two of them have on bright orange flight suits! It's them! They found the scientists! They found the scientists!"

Brown stepped outside the opening to clear the way for the others. As he did, Starr and DeArman popped through, with the scientists right behind them. "Get to your fighter and stand ready!" yelled Starr. "As soon as your guys are aboard, lift off. Don't wait for us."

"I'm already there." yelled DeArman.

One scientist went with DeArman while the other followed Starr. Scrambling up the ladder, Starr shoved the man through the hatch and pointed to the seat belts attached to the floor. She followed him in and got to her seat. As she did she glanced down to see a familiar face smiling up at her. "Verna! Is it really you?"

"For the moment, David," she smiled. "We're not out of the woods just yet."

One by one each of the team members emerged and raced toward their ships, leaving Johns and Brown to bring up the rear. Johns fired blindly into the tunnel a few times, then shouted, "Let's go, son."

They ran to Starr's fighter and reaching the bottom of the ladder, Johns stopped and turned around to face the tunnel. "We've got to keep them pinned down long enough for the others to get to their ship."

"Pin who down, Captain?"

Then as they looked at the tunnel opening Johns began firing and screamed, "THEM!"

"Whoa! What the heck are those things?" Brown yelled back.

"Just shoot… and keep shooting. Don't let them get out of the tunnel." Starr's ship was the closest which meant they had to provide cover for the others as they bolted to the other Vindicator.

As the last man made it to DeArman's ship, Starr told Johns and Brown to get inside. She would take it from here. Just as they made it safely inside, the opening to the tunnel seemed to explode as hundreds of "things" began pouring out and charged the Vindicators. Starr aimed her cannon at the opening and began chewing her way through a horde of horrifying creatures. She dropped them like flies, but they still kept charging. "My God!" she thought. "It's like an ant mound. They just keep coming by the thousands!"

"Ants?" Johns questioned. "What kind of ants are as big as a Rottweiler, weight 200 pounds and have teeth like a piranha?"

"Well, whatever they are, I don't like them!"

"Heavy D to Rocket Babe. We're lifting off…now!" Starr watched the other Vindicator streak into the sky.

"Hang on," she commanded, as she ignited her engine. They all heard a dual pop as they blazed into the sky. Looking back down Starr could see the descent stage crawling with those "things." Just looking at them gave her the shivers. "Nasty little bugs! I hate bugs!" Then she ordered, "Brown, blow it now!"

Brown pushed the little white button on his remote and 200 pounds of TNT closed the tunnel and killed dozens of the Martian ants. In a second or two, everyone on board could hear rocks and dirt pinging the sides and bottom of the fighter, while Starr saw debris and "bug" parts flying past her window. Johns asked Starr if they were supposed to be getting hit by all of that stuff. She quietly said, "No, but we seem to be above it now and the systems are showing nominal. I think we're ok."

Starr and Heavy D continued to climb, and as they did she radioed Lutz and Thomas. "Rocket Babe to Falcon. Launch and detonate!"

"Roger, Rocket Babe. On the way!"

Several miles away she saw them rising above the Pyramid and then a bright flash as they blew their explosives. "Rocket Babe to Pandora. Everyone is outbound and headed for home!"

"Roger, Rocket Babe. Outbound for home."

Now well into the thin Martian atmosphere, Verna could see Heavy D's fighter exactly where he should be, in the wingman's position. But as they reached the 20 mile mark she began to see a thin vapor trail streaming behind him.

"Heavy D… Check your fuel level."

"Roger, Rocket Babe. My fuel level is… not good. Something is wrong. I'm already down to 40% and we're not even half way."

"You probably caught a rock from the blast or something."

"We're not going to make it. We'll make 40 miles at best and even

I know they can't bring Pandora that low. She would buckle trying to break orbit."

"No, Major, we're all going to make it. I'll get you to 60 miles. Just continue max thrust until your fuel is completely gone, but hold your RCS in reserve... and standby."

"Roger, Rocket Babe. Max thrust. Standing by."

"Rocket Babe to Pandora... "

"Pandora, this is Ryan."

"Tell the commander we have a problem. Heavy D is losing fuel rapidly and we need to act quickly to save them."

"Standby, Rocket Babe." Ryan turned to the commander and began to explain, but Jackson cut him off.

"I heard her, Mister Ryan. Ask her how she wants to proceed."

"Aye, sir. Rocket Babe, Commander wants to know how you want to proceed."

"Good! Tell Connor to maintain his present course but lower the ship's orbit to 60 miles and have the other fighters adjust their courses accordingly. I'll get Heavy D to 60 miles and we'll rendezvous on this pass. There won't be enough time for another try."

Commander Jackson stared at the forward viewer a few seconds, then at Connor. "Seriously?" asked Connor. "You want me to take us to the edge of the upper atmosphere? How's she going to get Heavy D to 60 miles? What is she thinking sir? How is she calculating all of this on the fly? It's crazy! She might kill them all; maybe us too!"

Jackson glanced at Collins then went back to the main viewer without responding to Connor's comments. After he thought another second or two he said, "Mr. Connor, take Pandora to 60 miles. Mr. Ryan, tell the other pilots to do the same... then tell Starr... we're on the way."

"Aye, sir...Pandora to Rocket Babe. Commander says you are go for 60 miles."

"Roger. 60 miles. Rocket Babe, out."

Rocket Babe

Now at 38 miles up, Verna could see the plume of Heavy D's engine begin to flicker and then it was gone. "Rocket Babe. Fuel at zero. Now what?"

"Ok, Major. Listen carefully. I want you to coast a bit and let's see how far you can get on your own. In the mean time, think back to when you were in flight school. Have you ever heard of USAF pilot, Robinson Risner?"

"No, Captain, I don't think so."

"Well, fortunately for you, Major, I have. Back in 1952, Risner and his wingman were flying escort for a group of fighter bombers during the Korean War when his wingman's fuel tank was hit by flak. Not wanting him to bail out far behind enemy lines, Risner flew behind his wingman and placed the nose of his jet against the rear of his wingman's plane then pushed him 60 miles to safety.

During the Viet Nam War another pilot, Captain Bob Pardo, performed a similar maneuver when his wingman was hit by flak on a bombing run. The wingman dropped his tail hook and Pardo used his windscreen to push him to safety. The maneuver is now called the Pardo Push, and now I'm going to do something similar for you that will come to be known as the Starr Lift. I'm going to come under your ship and place the lip of my top hatch inside the bell of your engine and lift you to 70 miles or higher."

"70 miles?" DeArman asked. "Why?"

"Because Major, I don't have the fuel to get us to 60 miles with the speed to match Pandora. Once we're at 70 miles or better we'll use Mars' gravity and our thrusters to attain rendezvous speed."

"Do you really think it will work, Captain?"

"I wouldn't try it if I didn't, Major, and besides, we won't have all the air turbulence Risner and Pardo had to deal with. All you have to do is tell everyone to hold on, be still and enjoy the ride."

"Are you kidding? We're packed in like sardines now. We won't be dancing in here."

"Glad to hear it. Looks like you're topping out about 42 miles, Major. You're beginning to lose speed now, so we need to get on with it."

"I just have one question, Captain. Will you have enough fuel to make it, too?"

"Of course, Major, with ounces to spare. I'm moving under you now."

Looking up through her docking window Starr maneuvered beneath him and in just a few seconds DeArman felt a gentle nudge as Starr's fighter began to lift his craft higher and faster. Slowly coaxing her engine up to max thrust she was able to maintain constant contact but even with the latest and much improved higher thrust engines, it took several minutes longer than normal to attain the altitude and speed needed to reach low orbit and Pandora.

"Heavy D, we're approaching our target. Keep your fingers crossed."

"No problem, I'll cross my eyes if that will help."

Starr watched her altimeter pass 60 miles, then 65 and finally as they broke 70 miles, Starr shut down her engine and tapped her RCS to allow the ships to part and get some distance. "Ok, Major, you can exhale now. We're a little over 72 miles!" The faces that had been so tense the last 15 minutes were now all smiles.

Turning her attention back to her radar she said, "Heavy D, it looks like we're in luck. I see something large headed our way. I have Pandora at 300 miles and closing. I've done all I can. The rest is up to you. We have to increase our speed by almost 900 miles per hour to match theirs. I'm going to take us down in front of the ship so they can overtake us. When they break 100 miles, we'll go. Just stay on me and you'll be fine."

"Trust me, Captain. I'll be on you like white on rice."

"Ok, maybe not that close, Major."

"Heavy D standing by…"

"Rocket Babe to Pandora. Request permission to come aboard."

"Pandora here. Permission granted."

Starr hesitated just a moment before saying "And Ryan, tell Major Knowles to set the barriers and close the backdoor."

"Roger. Close the backdoor."

Immediately Collins was on the comlink to Knowles. "XO to CAG. Set crash condition in the bays."

"Knowles. Acknowledged!"

Verna watched the radar until Pandora came within 100 miles, then hit her thrusters. With their speed rapidly climbing DeArman stayed right beside her as all three ships converged on an empty point in space. Watching the Pandora grow larger by the second, Verna began calling out their speed. "Now at 7700...7800...7900, speed 8,000, shut down now!" As they merged into Pandora's flight path, Star said, "Not bad, Major. You make an excellent wingman. Our speed is 8,035 mph. Let's get a better view of the ship." And with that they rotated around and flew backwards so they could monitor the ship's approach.

"Pandora to Rocket Babe. We have you on visual. Hold your course."

"Roger, Pandora. Holding course."

"Ok, Major, just make a normal approach and let's try to set them in easy. Major Knowles won't like it if you stretch the net."

As the ship caught up with them they used their thrusters to set down gently on deck. Starr breathed a sigh of relief. "Nicely done, Major. Let's hope this is the last time we ever have to land backwards."

"Amen, Captain. I'll second that!"

"Rocket Babe, this is Major Knowles. Please stand by while we recover the remaining fighters then report to decon. Dr. Patel is waiting for all of you."

"Rocket Babe, acknowledged."

As soon as all the fighters were secured and the bay pressurized, everyone made their way to the decontamination area to be examined by Patel. Commander Jackson arrived as they were going into decon and he told Patel to take care of Starr and the scientists first. As soon as all three were released, Jackson met them at the door and told them to come with him. Once they were in the ready room, Jackson praised Starr for her leadership and a tremendous rescue effort. Verna thanked him and began the formal introductions. "Commander Jackson, this is David Miller, owner and CEO of Sirius and this is his lead scientist, Rolf Stabroth."

Jackson shook their hands, looked at her a moment, and said, "Captain, from the tone of your introduction you sound as though you already know these gentlemen."

"Well sir… that's because I do. I've known them for several years."

Jackson shook his head and said, "Why am I not surprised?" Turning to them he began, "Gentlemen, Starr and I have to get back to the bridge but Major Knowles and his men will see to all of your needs until we can get back to you. I want to hear every detail of your ordeal and what you've learned about the Greys, but first we have to complete our mission."

Miller replied, "We understand Commander. We'll look forward to speaking with you soon."

As they started toward the bridge, Jackson told Starr that as soon as she was ready to increase Pandora's orbit to 500 miles and bring the targeting console online. "I want this over on the next pass, understood?"

"Aye, sir. Understood."

Collins was standing next to the door waiting for Verna to step onto the bridge, and as she did he grabbed her and hugged her tight. "That was amazing, Captain. Congratulations!"

"Well, thank you, sir, but if it's ok, I still need oxygen to breath."

Releasing her and stepping back a bit, he said, "I'm sorry, Captain. I'm just glad and excited to have you back."

Verna looked at him and said, "We were only gone a few hours,

Bill, and I told you we'd be back. Have I ever lied to you?"

Collins smiled at her saying, "No, Captain. I can't say you have."

As she began strapping in, Connors quietly praised her. "Congratulations, Captain. Well done. I have to admit, I had my doubts."

"Thank you, Major, but I had a lot of help. And thanks for coming to retrieve us." Verna took her station and told the commander she was ready.

Jackson looked at Ryan and nodded. "You have ship wide, sir."

"All hands, this is the commander. Stand by for powered flight."

Starr reached for her joy stick and announced, "My board shows green, going in 3... 2... 1... ignition. Now!" Verna brought the engines up at 20% and maintained thrust for almost five minutes. "Commander, we are now at 500 miles altitude and cruising at 20,500 mph. Our current course will bring us directly over primary targets in 15 minutes." Then pressing the little red button on her flight console for the very first time, she watched as the targeting screen appeared on her monitor. The heads up display now projected the planet in relation to their orbit, as it tracked the ground targets. Once she had confirmed the information on the screen, Verna said, "We're ready, Commander. All we need are the access codes for the nukes. Yours first; then Mr. Collins; then mine."

"Very well, Captain. My code is 1936816." Verna watched as the first light on the screen flashed green three times, and then remained solid indicating the code had been accepted.

"Mr. Collins. Your code, please."

"My code is 3121576." Almost instantly the second light flashed green three times and remained solid. Finally, Jackson and Collins looked on as Starr input her code, 7152000. This time the green light flashed three times and went solid and as it did the word ARMED appeared in large red letters.

"I have code confirmation, sir. All nukes are hot. Fifteen minutes to optimum firing arch."

Commander Jackson eased over to Starr's station. "This is your big day, Captain. You get to sit in my chair. Exchange seats with me."

"Excuse me, sir?"

"I'm promoting you to acting commander. Go sit in my chair."

"But why, sir?"

"Because, Captain, we are about to nuke an entire species out of existence, and 60 years down the road I don't want you to have that on your conscience. I'm the commander. It's my responsibility. Now move." To this point no one had thought about what Jackson had just said. They really were about to extinguish an entire race.

The bridge fell silent as Starr reluctantly moved to the commander's chair and Jackson settled into hers. Then talking to no one in particular he said, "As hostile as they are, they are a life form, and it is regrettable that this is necessary. But in order to protect our own species, we must end them."

A few seconds later the targets on the screen flashed red and a bell began to sound. Jackson announced, "Targets acquired. Launching ground penetrating nukes 1 through 4 in 5... 4... 3... 2... 1."

Jackson looked down at the console and flipped 4 switches forward then pressed the red button. At that moment the Pandora became many tons lighter as the missiles dropped away from the ship and headed for their targets. Quietly they all watched the main viewer as the missiles closed on their targets. Two minutes later, blinding white flashes erupted on the areas known as The Face, the Pyramid, The Fortress and The City.

With a very thin atmosphere and low gravity, debris that wasn't vaporized flew away from the blast zones fast enough to reach escape velocity. Four 180 million °F detonations, well under ground and only a few miles apart, began to form what would become the largest individual crater on the surface of Mars, and when it cooled it would be completely lined by red glass. The bridge crew sat and watched the monitor as a giant Mach 2 dust storm roared across the surface in all directions. In only a few hours, it would shroud the entire surface of Mars for years to come.

A few minutes later, Major Driskill contacted the bridge to let them know main radar had been restored and the ship was now back to 100 percent. "Thank you, Major," replied Jackson. "What is the status of the Vindicators?"

"We'll have them all ready to go within the hour, sir."

"Let me know when you are finished, Major. I want to get resupplied and start for home ASAP."

"We're on it, sir. Driskill out."

"Starr, how long until we rendezvous with the supply ship?"

"Whenever you want, sir. I put us in this orbit so all we would need to do is catch up. It's orbiting at the same speed and altitude we are, just on the opposite side of the planet. We can catch it in just a few minutes."

"Do it."

"Aye, sir."

Ryan interrupted them, "Excuse me, sir, but we may have a problem. I'm not sure."

"What is it? Radar out again?"

"No, sir. It's what's on the radar that concerns me."

"Well, what is it? Speak up!"

"Well sir, SRN is showing two objects closing on the planet from opposite directions. One is very large. The other is very fast."

"Spit it out, man. Give the tactical for both."

"The largest is approximately 2 miles across; speed 30,000 mph. The other one is following our original course to Mars and its speed is 92,000 mph."

"What?" Jackson asked in stunned amazement. "Starr, what's the fastest speed ever recorded for an alien ship?"

"According to HQ, the fastest ship they have ever tracked was approximately 60,000 mph."

"Ryan, what are their ETA's?"

"If they both maintain present course and speed, the larger one will reach the planet in approximately 6 hours. The other one will arrive less than an hour later, sir."

"Starr, get us to the resupply ship. Ryan, tell Driskill and Knowles to drop what they're doing and prepare for resupply operations."

Chapter 13

Five hours later, Driskill notified the Commander that he and Major Knowles had completed the resupply operation. "Good work, Major. Not a moment too soon. How are you coming with the Vindicators?"

"They're ready to go too, sir."

"Thank you, Major. Ryan... ship wide."

"Go ahead, sir."

"Commander to all hands.... As you all know, we have a pair of unidentified ships moving at high speed to intercept Pandora. Maintain alert status and be prepared to go to general quarters. Obviously, we have no idea what we'll be facing over the next few hours. I want the pilots in their Vindicators and ready to launch on a moment's notice. Stand by."

Starr started to get up and report to the launch bay but Jackson told her to stay put. "I'm sorry, sir. I thought you said you wanted the pilots in their fighters."

"Not you. Knowles has it covered. This time you're staying here." Verna sat back down and continued watching her monitor.

"The large ship is now matching our speed and coming into visual range sir, on main viewer... now."

On the screen, they saw a huge black triangle shaped ship, slowly rotating counter clockwise. "What... is... that?" Connor asked.

"Give me what you have, Ryan."

"Aye, sir. Distance 25 miles and closing. Radar shows the alien ship is 2,000 feet per side, 500 feet from top to bottom. No sign of a portal, hatch, or entrance of any kind. I'm not detecting a heat source or engine emissions. Hull is impenetrable and I cannot identify anything that we would call a bridge or detect any signs of life. There are no distinguishing surface features. Computer estimates gross weight in excess of 25 million tons."

As they sat waiting for something to happen, the triangular ship continued to rotate. Two sides had gone around before Starr finally caught a glimpse of something she recognized. "Look!" she shouted. "Ryan, magnify the leading edge of the right corner." Ryan increased the magnification by five, and Starr said, "Oh... this is not good!"

"What is it?" Jackson asked.

"It's a name plate and... it's in Greek, Latin, and Hebrew."

"What? Can you read it... what does it say?"

"Of course sir, it says... Nephilim."

"Nephilim? What the heck is that?" asked Fontaine.

"Not a what, but a who," replied Starr.

Jackson looked at her and said, "Explain, Captain."

"The Nephilim and their descendants were mentioned several places in the Bible, sir. Some passages refer to them as 'giants' believed to be the sons of God and daughters of men. The Hebrew word 'naphal' is a verb meaning to fall. Some Biblical scholars believe the Nephilim to be the children of the fallen angels. Genesis 6 says, and I quote:

> Now it came about, when men began to multiply on the face of the land and daughters were born to them, that the sons of God, bene Elohim, saw that the daughters of men were beautiful. And they took wives for themselves whomever they chose. Then the Lord said, "My Spirit shall not strive with man forever, because he also is flesh; nevertheless his days shall be one hundred and twenty years." The Nephilim were on the earth in those days, and also afterward, when the sons of God came in to the daughters of men, and they bore children to them. Those were the mighty men who were of old, men of renown. Then the Lord saw that the wickedness of man was great on the earth, and that every intent of the thoughts of his heart was only evil continually. (NASB)

"Back then, they ranged in height from 12 to 35 feet; literally giants to humans. Skeletal remains have been found on almost every continent over the last 400 years. If that is who we're facing, I advise not going hand to hand."

Then what sounded like a male voice came over their com-system and stated, "We have been observing you since you arrived and know all that has transpired on your ship and the planet you call Mars. We know of your actions in the tunnels and what you have done below. The female you call Starr is correct. We are the descendants of the Nephilim. We were too far away and you have destroyed almost all of our 'little ones.' Now you must account for your actions."

"Where's that coming from, Ryan? How are they using our own system?"

"I don't know, sir, but they have cut in somehow. It's going all over the ship, sir, and I can't figure out how to stop it."

"If you can hear me, this is Commander Jackson of the U.S.S. Pandora. Your 'little ones' had been raiding our planet for centuries, terrorizing us, abducting and experimenting on our people, and we now have the power to stop them and any other race that is a threat to us, and so we have. It's that simple. We came here to deal with them and any other race that has been raiding Earth. Are you the ancient race Starr told us about from the Bible?"

"Yes, we can hear you, and the female has been correct about many things she has told you. I am Anakim. Our forefathers have visited your planet many times and will again. They helped your kind build great structures. They helped build great cities. They mingled with your people and made wives of them. Many of their descendants are on our home world now and other planets and moons nearby. You call our home Titan."

"How is it that you speak our language so well?"

"We know many tongues. Many originated on your home world. Some of the tongues you know were given to your ancestors by our ancestors."

"Then you must know what they had been doing to humans. Yet you allowed all of it to happen."

"After we conquered those you call Greys, they served us well for many centuries. We therefore allowed them their curiosities. They brought us servants and wives and many other things but now they are gone, and those on your ship and their descendents will take their places, or we will destroy you all."

"Commander, they're coming along side of us; distance one mile."

"Sound general quarters, Mr. Ryan. Starr, bring the Phoenix missiles online."

"What should I target, sir?"

"I don't know, Captain. Just pick a spot and stand by."

"Aye, sir, but that ship is so big. I'm not sure we'll have much effect on it using conventional weapons."

"Nephilim ship, this is Commander Jackson. I will only say this once. Break orbit and withdraw."

"You make us laugh, Commander. We are much larger, much stronger than you, both our physical bodies and our ship. You are like insects to us. Our weapons are fearsome, able to tear apart entire planets! You are no match for us on any level, but we will say this only once as well. Send me the female, Starr, that I may know her. Then serve us, and we will spare your lives. What is your response?"

"Ryan, tell CAG to launch the Vindicators... Nephilim ship, Captain Starr will respond to your demands herself. Explain our position to them, Captain."

"Aye, sir. Launching Phoenix missiles now."

The forward launch bay of the bridge opened and a pair of Phoenix missiles rocketed toward the Nephilim ship. As they cleared the tube, one arched high over the center of the ship while the other swung below to strike from the underside. Everyone on the bridge watched the missiles as they completed their course, with Starr counting down to impact, 3... 2...1. She had programmed them perfectly and they arrived together, precisely in the center of the ship, top and bottom. There was a flash of red light above and below as the missiles exploded into the Nephilim hull causing fragments of an unknown material to fly into space. There were two large, jagged holes where the missiles struck, but as she watched for signs they had hit something critical the triangular ship continued to rotate at the same rate as before. Starr looked at Jackson and said, "We're going to need quite a few more of those to slow them down, sir. I estimate 70 to 75. There really isn't any point in launching the Sidewinders or Sparrows."

Jackson's only response was, "Understood."

The Vindicators flew across the topside of the massive ship strafing the hull as they went, but the pilots saw no effect as their rounds seemed to bounce right off and into space.

"Heavy D to Pandora. We're having no effect, sir. We've made two runs and concentrated our fire in a single area, but can't seem to penetrate the hull at all."

Jackson thought a moment, and then told Ryan to recall the fighters.

"Pandora to Heavy D. Bring them home."

"Aye, sir. Heavy D, out."

"Mr. Ryan, tell Knowles to get the Vindicators secured as fast as possible." Turning to Collins he ordered, "XO, prepare the ship for powered flight."

"Aye, sir! This is the XO. All hands standby for powered flight."

"Starr, arm the nukes!"

"Sir?"

"Arm the nukes! All of them! And target the Nephilim ship. Do you need the codes again?"

"No, sir!" Starr's fingers were a blur on her console and in an instant she said, "Nukes armed and ready, sir!" Jackson nodded to her and waited for her to say they were ready to launch.

As Verna waited for all the lights on her board to turn green, Ryan solemnly said, "Commander, the second ship is coming into visual range. It has slowed considerably, but there's something strange, sir. Now it's squawking a DSSF code."

"It's what?"

"I'm getting a DSSF fighter code, and sir, you need to check the main view screen." Jackson looked to see a ship shaped like a fighter with the exact same bridge as the Pandora, with DSSF markings and twin Jolly Rogers on the tails.

Suddenly Ryan heard, "This is Randall in command of the DSSF Fighter, Cestris. Tell Commander Jackson I need to speak to Scheherazade."

"The commander of the Cestris ship is calling us, sir, and you by name."

"Well, put him on!"

Starr turned to Jackson and began to smile knowingly. "What is it Captain?"

"It's the cavalry, sir."

"The what?"

"Sir, he wants to speak to… Scheherazade."

"Who?"

Verna's smile brightened as she excitedly said, "That's what he calls me, sir. I'm Scheherazade."

"Who calls you?"

"My other half, sir." A look of understanding came over Jackson's face as he told Ryan to put him on.

"Go ahead, Cestris. Captain Starr is here."

"Verna, I need you to move the Pandora, now!"

"I knew you would come and none too soon."

"We can talk later. Right now I need you to get the Pandora out of orbit as rapidly as possible."

"What course?"

"Continue on your present course until you reach escape velocity.

The Nephilim will follow you and when they do, I'll come around and take them out as you break away for Earth. But you have to be above 30,000 mph when I fire or the blast will take Pandora down as well."

"How? With what, a nuke?"

"I don't have time to explain now. Just get moving and don't look back!"

"What about you… What about the Nephilim ship?"

"Leave them to me. Just get the Pandora on course to Earth and at maximum speed."

Starr stared at Jackson and he said, "How long until we can get moving?"

"We're ready now, sir."

"Then count it down and let's go!"

"Aye, sir…This is Captain Starr. All hands prepare for powered flight in 3… 2… 1."

Just as the engines ignited, the Nephilim fired what appeared to be a laser beam at the Pandora, striking the leading edge of the starboard launch bay. It only took the beam two seconds to burn a jagged hole four feet in diameter all the way through the bay, and as it rapidly decompressed the acrylic glass doors shattered out into space. The impact and reaction caused the Pandora to roll almost 90 degrees to that side, but Starr managed to right the ship and keep the Pandora on course.

"Damage report, Mr. Ryan."

"Knowles reports starboard launch bay has a huge hole all the way through the deck, and the doors are gone but no casualties."

"Good. Tell him to hang tight."

The Pandora's sudden departure had caught the Nephilim off guard, but they quickly began to pursue and as they did Randall had the Cestris alter course and speed to intercept them on the opposite side of the planet. He intended to make a head on run at them as the Pandora sped away. The huge ship could not accelerate as quickly as the Pandora, and as it began to fall behind it fired again. This time the beam removed the number 2 fin and part of the fairing. Two feet to the right and they would have nailed the main fuel tank. Feeling the strike, Starr nudged her throttles to 25% and prayed they would reach their course transition point in time. Ryan checked the radar and reported, "They're falling behind sir. Distance between ships is now 10 miles."

They fired again on the Pandora, and the beam hit another fin, clipping off the end. But this time there was less reaction by the Pandora as the beam struck the ship. Starr turned to Jackson and together they said, "The weapon has a limited range!"

Jackson caught his breath and said, "Let's see if we can slow them down a bit, Captain. Set a nuke on a 10 second delay and release it behind us."

Hurriedly Starr flipped a switch and said, "Nuke, away!" Watching the aft view screen, everyone on the bridge waited to see how the alien ship would be affected. The bomb drifted down and under the Nephilim ship, then detonated about a quarter mile behind it. The flash that followed blinded the view for the Pandora for a few seconds, but when the focus returned they could see the far side of the Nephilim ship glowing orange like a blast furnace, but still in pursuit of the Pandora!

Ryan checked his radar again and stated, "Not only is there no discernible damage, they're now overtaking us."

Starr held steady as their speed gradually increased. Now at 28,000 mph and almost to the breakaway point in their orbit, she told them to be prepared to go to max thrust. Collins looked at Ryan and asked, "Where's the Cestris?"

"They're turning inbound on us now from our 2 o'clock, sir."

On board the Cestris, Randall was setting up for the kill.

"Penelope, time and distance to target?"

"Distance is 1,000 miles and 31 seconds, sir."

"Addison. Maintain course and speed."

"Aye, sir."

"Sela, arm two Eradicators and standby to fire."

"Armed and ready, sir."

Randal watched the main viewer as the targeting computer cross hairs merged to a single point in space. "Steady...steady... *now* Sela! Light 'em up!"

Sela quickly pushed the red button on her weapons station twice... "Torpedoes away!"

"Addison, hard to starboard. Go to max thrust and get us out of here!"

"Aye, sir!"

On board the Pandora, Ryan's alarm went off as his radar picked up a pair of fast moving objects headed in their direction. "Sir, I have a pair of torpedoes headed straight for us... speed 35,000 mph."

Jackson responded with a questioning tone... "Starr?"

"We're fine, sir. He's not targeting us. Pandora speed now 30,000 mph... Standby to break orbit in 3...2...1... now!" And with that Starr pushed the throttles to 60% just as the Eradicators passed over them only 50 feet above. Less than a second later there was a cataclysmic explosion as the torpedoes penetrated the Nephilim ship, ripping through it like a mighty dagger. On the aft view screen, they could see a burst of fire erupt on top of the ship as the Eradicators impacted the hull. Less than two seconds later from beneath the ship streamed twin jets of debris, as tons of unidentified material flowed from the bowels of the ship. The Nephilim attempted to fire their beam one last time, but just as they did the ship exploded like a super nova.

The Cestris had completely destroyed the massive ship, but in its place was a rapidly expanding shell of pure energy that was devouring everything in its path. Watching the shell expand behind them Ryan struggled to get out, "It's closing on us, Commander. Energy field moving at 42,000 mph; distance is less than ten miles; impact in 30 seconds."

Collins asked, "What happens if that... catches us?"

At that point Starr pushed all five engines to 104% in hopes they might out run it. Pandora was now at 40,000 mph but the energy shell was still closing on them. Ryan continued to watch the screen but as he did he noticed it was beginning to dissipate and after a few seconds he yelled, "Commander, it's losing strength!"

"How long to impact?"

"That's a negative on impact, sir. We're now exceeding the energy field's speed, sir. I think we will out run it."

That was great news, but Starr thought it best they continue at 104% until they reached 60,000 mph. It took a few minutes to reach that speed, but finally Starr shut down the engines as the event fell far behind them. After a few seconds passed, she suddenly remembered the Cestris and asked Ryan if he could locate them on radar. Ryan watched a few sweeps across his screen, and then said, "I'm not seeing anything on Pandora radar. Switching to SRN." But after more than a minute he finally said, "I'm sorry, Captain. I can't find them. I suppose they might have gone behind Mars to escape the energy field."

"Hail them," Jackson ordered.

"U.S.S. Pandora to Cestris. Come in please." Several seconds went by and Ryan tried again. "Pandora to Cestris. Please respond." After a few tense moments, Ryan said, "I'm sorry Captain. There's no response."

Starr looked at Jackson as tears filled her eyes and begged, "We've got to go back. They could have crash landed on Mars or Phobos and need our help."

Collins looked at Jackson for his decision. "Are we going back, sir?"

Jackson hesitated, thinking of the possible consequences and said, "I want to go back. I do, but... they should be on radar, unless..." Starr slowly turned in her seat and faced forward as her entire body trembled. Tears streamed down her cheeks as she dropped her head and silently struggled for breath. She remained that way for a minute or so, then finally raised her head and stared blankly out the starboard window into space. As she did she caught a glimpse of something outside the ship. She blinked her eyes clear to see better and saw a large white object fill her view. Not sure what she was seeing she ripped off her seat belts in one quick motion and scrambled to the window for a better look.

"What are you doing, Captain?" Jackson asked. He was concerned that she might have 'lost it' and was going to try to jump through the window.

As she got to the glass and stood fully in the window, she saw another ship emerging from under the Pandora, and there on the fuselage she could plainly see S.S. Cestris. Over in the port window of the Cestris stood Randall, slowly waving at her. She frantically waved back as the tears stopped and her usual bright smile returned to her face. As she stood with her back to the others and blocking the window, the rest of the crew thought she had clearly lost her mind. Jackson looked at Collins for some idea of how to handle her. Starr stepped back, and turning to Jackson screamed, "They're alive! They're alive!"

Jackson got up to see for himself, and as he got to the window he could see the same thing: a man on the Cestris, waving at them. "Unbelievable. They are alive!"

Collins came to have a look, as did Fontaine, Ryan and Connor. "Son of a...where did they come from?"

"Evidently, they were tucked in beneath Pandora, sir."

Ryan apologized and said, "I'm sorry, sir. I'm sorry, Captain Starr. I guess I lost track of them watching the energy shell."

Verna looked at Randall across the way and said, "The sneaky little Indian. Scared me to death! Wait until I get my hands on you!"

As the surprise of it all began to wear off, Starr turned to Jackson and asked permission for Randall to come aboard. "Permission granted, Captain. In fact, Mr. Ryan, issue a personal invitation from me to the entire crew of the Cestris to join us for dinner, then send them our docking code."

"Aye, sir. Contacting them now."

"Would you like to oversee docking procedures, Captain?"

"Yes, sir!"

Jackson, smiling at Starr said, "I've heard and seen things on this mission I never dreamed of and I'm looking forward to meeting your 'other half' and finally hearing how all of this actually came about. He must be quite a man."

"I think he is, sir. I'm sure you'll like him." Not long after, the Cestris crew was on board the Pandora.

Starr anxiously waited for Randall by the port window as Collins and Jackson stood at Ryan's station, whispering about the "imminent reunion" they were about to witness. Ryan said, "From what I've seen from Starr to date, I've got a month's pay that says there won't be much to it. Starr will be very reserved and show little emotion, if any at all. I mean, what man could possibly live up to her standards? I doubt she could have real feelings for a man that would let her join DSSF and be away for so long and in such dangerous situations."

Collins laughed at Ryan's prediction and said, "I'll cover your month's pay. Watch and learn Lieutenant. I believe when she sees him, she's going to scream with excitement and run and jump into his arms. Then they will kiss and her left foot will rise off the floor behind her."

Ryan laughed back and said, "You're on, sir!"

Hearing voices approaching the bridge, Jackson said, "And now for the moment of truth."

As Randall stepped onto the bridge, Commander Jackson looked at Starr and said, "Captain, I believe you have a visitor."

Verna whirled from the window to see Randall smiling at her with his arms out. Her heart literally skipped a beat as a brilliant smile covered her face, almost as fast as she covered the distance between them. The weightless environment could do little to slow her down.

With her ears ringing and practically breathless, just as Collins had said, they fell together and held a long passionate kiss... as her left foot lifted from the floor. In a moment or two, Connor, Fontaine, Collins, and Jackson all began to clap. Ryan just stood there in amazement.

After what seemed like more than enough time, Commander Jackson cleared his throat as Verna came up for air. Looking up into Randall's eyes she said, "You feel really good. I may never let you go." Jackson cleared his throat a little louder and waited for the pair to part. Finally, Verna stepped back slightly and said, "I'm sorry, Commander. I guess I got a little excited."

"Perfectly understandable, Captain, but please, introduce me to your friend."

"Commander Jackson, I would like to present my fiancé, Randall, the man whose ship took down the Nephilim."

Putting out his hand Jackson offered, "I'm pleased to meet you, Randall. We've heard... very little about you... to this point."

Shaking his hand Randall replied, "I'm pleased to meet you, too, Commander. Thank you for the invitation to come aboard. Hello, Bill. You're looking well. You've been hitting the MRE's kinda hard haven't you?" Collins rolled his eyes and complained about the lack of available exercise space on board. "I'm just kidding you, Bill. Good to see you again."

"We are happy to have you and your crew on the Pandora," Jackson said. "I can't wait to hear all about your ship... and your amazing weaponry. What kind of warhead was that?"

Randall looked a little confused and said, "We were monitoring your communications and know that you rescued David and Rolli. Haven't you talked to them?"

"Actually, with everything that has happened since they came aboard, we haven't had the time."

At that moment, Major Knowles arrived with the rest of the Cestris crew. "Commander, allow me to introduce my crew. This is my radar and communications specialist, Penelope; our pilot, Addison; and my weapons officer, Sela."

The ladies all smiled as Jackson gently shook their hands and said, "Looks like DSSF is upgrading its staff. I have never seen such a lovely crew."

Ryan looked at Randall a moment and said, "Let me get this straight. Your entire crew is female?"

"That's right, but I do have one vacant position. I need a second in command."

Commander Jackson, looking a bit disappointed, said, "Let me guess who you have in mind," as Verna smiled and rolled her eyes.

Collins interrupted, "This has all been fascinating, gentlemen, but why don't we join Mr. Miller and Mr. Stabroth in the ready room and continue our conversation there?"

Jackson agreed. "Excellent idea, Mr. Collins. Let's do that."

Later in the ready room, over some MRE's and Kona coffee, the scientists explained the latest developments and current status of DSSF. Miller explained that the joint chiefs believed with all the recent advances in space based operations made by Sirius, and under the president's leadership, Russia and the Wall would collapse within a few years as they tried to keep up. That would leave the U.S. as the world's lone super power. The next great challenge would come from space, and it is coming now.

Jackson and Collins sat spell bound as Miller explained he had some good news and some bad news. "The bad news is that we now know there are many more alien races than we first thought, and they are coming for our resources and our people. It doesn't end with taking out the Greys' bases on Mars. That's only the first step in a long series of efforts we must make to protect the Earth and its people. From our satellites and SRN scans we also know the Nephilim are a much more serious threat than all the other aliens combined. The ship the Cestris took out was one of their small ones, and we have seen their kind on Earth as recently as last month. Most of them look very similar to humans, but they average more than 20 feet in height. HQ believes they are abducting women for breeding.

"The good news is that there are three additional Juno class battleships like Pandora entering service in less than 30 days, with more advanced ships beginning construction, and like the Cestris, they will be carrying the new Eradicator, anti-matter torpedoes. Unfortunately for us, Randall's ship is the prototype. It took us seven years to get it off the ground, but now that it's been proven in battle others will soon follow. You really need to visit Randall's ship, Commander. The bridge exterior may look similar to Pandora's, but inside they are vastly different. A standard crew of five has twice the space per individual. Each member has their own cabin and there is a real galley, with stores for one year. The armament is state of the art and she carries 30 Eradicator anti-matter torpedoes as well as a small complement of conventional missiles and a rail gun. The Cestris cruisers can operate for 15 years without refueling and perform like a jet in any atmosphere. So far the Cestris has only slightly exceeded 100,000 mph, but we believe with a little tweaking her speed can be doubled.

"DSSF plans to have 21 in service by the end of this year. We just need to train the pilots and we are already doing that. Rollie has built and designed the trainers and the software needed to produce great pilots before they have ever been to space. Starr was our first. She has a superior mind and abilities, but part of what makes her almost super human is her dedication to the training."

"Let me guess," said Jackson. "All female?"

"Almost," Miller responded.

"And that's because…?"

"Because women are usually more teachable, patient, and intuitive, Commander. You've worked with Starr for a while now. How many times has she saved your bacon? In the future we won't just be fighting brute strength against brute strength. We'll need pilots and soldiers that fight with their heads, and let the technology do the heavy lifting.

"Now, here's the worst part. With the planets aligning in 1984 and the distance between all of the planets being approximately as close as they get, HQ believes we may be fighting a war for survival on several fronts. I, for one, would expect the Nephilim to respond to the loss of their ship, and it is greatly feared that the aliens may try to re-establish a permanent outpost on Mars or Mercury or perhaps even the moon. We are at the very beginning, Commander, and it may be a long time before it's over."

Jackson shook his head in disbelief and said, "Gentlemen, this has been a great deal to take in for one evening, but I'm sure by the time we get back home we'll all feel better about the future. Now, if you'll excuse me, I think I'll turn in... And Starr, permission to leave the ship, but be at your station on time."

Verna smiled and said, "Thank you, sir!"

Later, as Randall gave Verna the guided tour of the Cestris, she could hardly believe her eyes. "This is amazing!" she exclaimed. "It's nice to have enough room to stretch and breathe again. Look at the size of your quarters and you even have a little nightstand!"

"There's plenty of room for two," he said.

"What? I don't get my own cabin?"

"If you like, but being second in command, it would be smaller. Wouldn't you rather share this one?"

"We're not married yet, mister!" Verna said with a laugh.

"We could be... Commander Jackson could do it. We could be the first couple married in space." Verna looked at him and said, "It does sound very romantic, but I want our parents to be with us. You understand, don't you?"

Randall looked a little frustrated, and then nodded his head. "Of course, I know Muggy would not be pleased if we were married without her present." Then he told her he had a surprise for her. "Look in the drawer of the nightstand." Pulling it open, Verna found a pearl handled brush and comb.

She smiled and said, "I love them! Over the next few days, as we have time, we can sit right here on the bed, shoes on of course, and while you brush my hair, we can plan the wedding all the way home."

"If I brush your hair, will you take it out of that silly bun and keep it down?"

"Are you serious?" she asked. "You know what happens to long hair in space. Maybe I should just go back to a pixie cut. If we're going to be on a ship all the time, that would be easier anyway." Randall just looked annoyed.

"Now, stop looking like you've lost your best friend and come sit with me." Randall sat on the bed with his back to the wall as Verna stretched out and snuggled up against him with her head on his chest. Once she was settled she softly said, "Sing to me."

"What should I sing?"

"I don't know; something romantic. Do you remember that old song we liked in eighth grade?"

Randall smiled and said, "Yes, I do." Then covering her with an old Cherokee blanket his grandmother had made many years ago, he began to sing softly as she drifted off to sleep.

Chapter 14

At an undisclosed location just thirty days after the Pandora bombed Mars, DSSF headquarters held a brief ceremony to recognize the participants of Operation Dust Storm. The President, General Barrett, and the Joint Chiefs were all in attendance to honor those who had taken part in the first ever combat mission on another world.

The speeches were eloquent and many ribbons, medals, and promotions were awarded. At the end of the ceremony two medals of honor were given, one posthumously, to Army Ranger Patrick J. Boyd, who gave his life to save the mission and many lives of his comrades. The second was awarded to Captain Verna L. Starr, for saving her ship and its crew multiple times during the mission. As the finale to the event, it was announced that as of that date DSSF would now be an extension of the U.S. Navy with all previous ranks converted as appropriate.

As Starr stood at attention for the President to place her medal of honor around her neck he said, "Captain Starr, in addition to your medal of honor, it is my pleasure to also give you your new insignia, as we promote you from Air Force Captain to Navy Captain, and in accordance with your promotion, you now have thirty days leave to consider your next assignment. You have the following three options to choose from for your next assignment: One, you may continue on the Pandora as third in command under Admiral Jackson and Commander Collins. Two, you may assume second in command duties on the Cestris, under Commander Randall. Three, you may assume command of the first production model of the Cestris class cruiser / interceptor and choose your own crew. Now, how does all that suit you, Captain?"

With a salute, Starr replied, "Right down to the ground, Mr. President." Then the President stepped back, smiled, and returned her salute.

At the party that followed, Verna congratulated all the others on their promotions. She was asked by Admiral Jackson if she knew which option she would choose. "I'm not sure, sir. I need some time to think about it. I never expected to have so many choices."

Verna saw Jackson glance at Randall, before saying, "You have more choices than you think. There are options other than DSSF, but I'm sure whatever you decide, it will be the right choice. Just remember, you are always welcome on the Pandora. Now go. Enjoy your leave."

"Thank you, sir, I will."

As Jackson walked away Verna turned to look for Randall and literally walked right into Captain Knowles.

"Well now, in a hurry are we, Miss?"

"Oh, I'm sorry, Mike. I was looking for Randall. What's up?"

"I was just coming to say congratulations on your promotion and your medal. Both are well deserved."

"Thank you, sir. Congratulations to you too!"

"So, will you stay with Pandora or sail away with 'him'?"

"I really don't know yet. There are too many options. And what about you? Will you stay with Commander…I mean, *Admiral* Jackson? You know how he depends on you."

"Without you as pilot, I just don't know. I'm not sure Connor can get us to the moon, much less deep space."

"Oh, come on Mike, you know Connor is a good pilot."

Knowles nodded his head in agreement, "Yes, he is, but he's no Rocket Babe."

Verna smiled and said, "And you don't want him to be. Just imagine what he'd look like in my dress whites and boots. He certainly doesn't have the legs for that."

"Oh no," Knowles said. "No, no, no!"

"Take care, Mike."

"You do the same. We'll be seeing each other again, I'm sure."

Again looking for Randall, she saw him standing with Commander Collins and as she walked up they stopped talking. "Oh, talking about me, were you?"

"Kind of. Bill was telling me I should kidnap you and make you marry me today."

"Is that so?"

"What I said was, you two shouldn't wait too long. That's all. There's no telling what may be coming down the road, you know. You two do realize this was the beginning, not the end. I just heard DSSF has increased its order from 21 to 50 Cestris class cruisers. They don't order that many if they don't need them. Development would be two or three at most. Fifty means they're expecting to need them... and soon. Mars was just the first salvo."

Thoughtfully Verna said, "I suppose that's true. There are several other races out there we might have to deal with Bill, but I have a suggestion for you, too."

"What's that?"

"Spend some time with your kids, and give Mary my love."

"I see. I'm being dismissed."

"Yes!"

"Fine, but if you two do get married, we expect an invitation."

"You and Mary will be first on the list. I promise." As Collins walked away Verna turned to Randall, hugged him and said, "Can we go, now? It's a long way to Rugby Avenue."

"That depends," he replied as he swung her around. "Are you going to wear your dress whites all the way home?"

Rolling her eyes she said, "Yes, just for you."

"Then yes, we can go now."

Two weeks later, Randall and Verna were sitting on her parents' sofa watching the Braves with her dad, when a special news report interrupted the game. A world famous astronomer was being interviewed and he began telling the reporter about the largest dust storm ever observed on Mars. It was his belief that approximately 30 days ago a small asteroid had impacted an area known as The City, blasting millions of tons of soil and rocks into the atmosphere. The ensuing dust cloud had now covered the entire surface of the planet, obscuring every feature.

Verna and Randall didn't even look at each other, pretending not to be interested in the story, but Muggy made the comment that she was glad Verna would not be going any further than Shepard Yard and besides, it was time she was starting a family. "Am I ever going to have any grandchildren?" Muggy asked. "I'm not getting any younger, you know."

Verna smiled and said, "Don't worry about me, Mom, and yes, you'll have them soon."

Nudging Randall, Muggy asked, "Do you even have anyone in mind?"

Almost giggling Verna said, "Actually I have several very good prospects but I think I'm going to stick with Randall. It would just be too much trouble to train another one."

Muggy raised her eyebrows at Randall, saying, "You know... if you were smart..."

Randall interrupted her and said, "You know I'm smart, but not too smart, right?"

"Yes, I do. You're just smart enough."

As the game came back on the phone rang, and after a few seconds her mom called Verna to the phone. "Verna Louise, its Captain Knowles, for you."

Verna looked at Randall and said, "This can't be good."

Handing her the phone Muggy whispered, "Don't you two run off anywhere. I'll have supper on the table in just a few minutes."

"Ok, Mom. We're not going anywhere right this minute. Hello? Mike?"

"Yes, Verna, this is Mike. I'm sorry to bother you at home and on leave but we have a situation and I need you and Randall back in Nevada, ASAP."

"What's going on, Captain?"

"It's best we talk face to face, Captain. There's a Phantom waiting for you at the 117th in Birmingham. It's fueled and ready to go. You're authorized to exceed Mach 2. Just drop your wing tanks over the Sheppard Air Force Base firing range. How soon can the two of you get to the 117th?"

"Give us an hour. We'll be there."

"Acknowledged! I'll let them know you're coming, and get Randall's dad to take you so you don't have to go through all the red tape."

"Ok, Mike. See you soon." Verna came back and told Randall they had to go right after supper and to call his dad to ask for a ride to the Guard.

Arriving at the 117th, Randall's dad flashed his I.D. at the guard then drove down to the flight line where they were greeted by Colonel James, who took them to their aircraft. Less than two hours later, Captain Knowles was waiting for them as they touched down at DSSF HQ.

Driving right up to the jet Knowles yelled up at them, "Hurry up you two. The general is waiting!"

They quickly climbed down from the plane and were barely in the back seat with the door closed when Knowles zipped off across the base. His departure caught her off guard and as he rounded a sharp curve, the turn forced her right up against Randall who quickly put an arm around her to keep her steady.

Verna yelled, "Dad gum it, Mike, where's the fire?"

"Don't worry, Captain. You'll see in just a few minutes."

Randall just smiled and said, "Oh, leave him alone. I can hold onto you no matter how fast he drives."

A look of suspicion came over her face as she said, "I see. Y'all are in on this together." But before either of them could answer the car screeched to a halt at the main door of the auditorium.

The trio entered the auditorium and found General Barrett standing next to a large projector talking on the phone. "Yes, Mr. President, they just arrived. I'll call you later with the latest news. Good bye, Mr. President."

As Barrett turned from the phone they all exchanged salutes, then he began by saying, "I'm sorry to cut your leave short, Captain, but when you see the film and hear what I have to say, I'm sure you'll understand the urgency of the situation. Knowles, dim the lights and show them the intel."

The screen flashed on and Captain Knowles began his narration, "We got this from SRN less than 5 hours ago and it is very disturbing!" When the film began they could see the now familiar triangular shape of a Nephilim ship and as it continued they saw ship after ship orbiting Saturn and its moons, Titan and Mimas. They continued watching as dozens of ships appeared around Jupiter and its moon, Ganymede, as well as Mars. "So far we have counted more than 200 Nephilim ships in various places."

"Are all of them as large as the one we fought?" Randall asked.

Turning from the screen, Barrett said, "Actually, that one was one of their smaller ships. More than half of the ships you see there are three times the size of the one you destroyed; more than six miles per side and one mile top to bottom. It seems we've stirred a very large hornet's nest, with some very large hornets."

Verna leaned over to Randall and quietly said, "More bugs!"

"More bugs, indeed," answered Barrett. "And what this film doesn't show are the 60 or more Grey ships that accompany them, and we are sure that we are not seeing every ship of the Nephilim fleet."

Knowles stopped the projector and turned the lights back on as Verna hesitatingly asked, "So how do we fit into the equation sir?"

"It's this simple, Captain. Given what we know to be their normal speed and considering the distances involved, it's possible that some portion of the Nephilim ships could be here in less than a month. In the meantime, we need pilots and crews trained to fly the Cestris class interceptors, and that's where you and Randall come in. Tomorrow morning you, Randall, and Captain Knowles will begin training the DSSF's top three rookie pilots. You will train Jack Purcell, Knowles will train Henry Purcell, and Randall will train Charles DeArman."

Verna thought a moment then said, "But General, it normally takes an experienced pilot a minimum of six months to fully adapt to a Vindicator, much less a Cestris class ship."

Barrett smiled and then replied, "And that's why you are here Captain. You have 30 days to get them ready."

Verna shook her head and mumbled under her breath, "Maybe, with 16 hour days and if they each had their own simulator and with Rollie's help, we might have them ready in three months…"

Barrett's tone didn't change as he said, "There are three simulators on base and Stabroth is set up and waiting on you and your team… and you have 30 days."

Looking at Barrett Verna asked, "Are Jack and Henry Purcell brothers? And is Charles the brother of Pandora pilot, Emmett DeArman?"

"That is correct," Barrett replied. "Now, Captain Knowles will show you to your quarters. Get a good night's sleep. The next few weeks will be long and hard."

As they walked down a long corridor Knowles smiled at Verna and said, "I told you we would be seeing each other again."

Verna half way smiled back and said, "Well, Mike, I had hoped it wouldn't be this soon."

Standing by the window, Verna looked up at the stars and sighed. Randall came and stood behind her, wrapping his arms around her tightly and said, "You know, if you are my second in command, what you wear will be up to you and you won't have to wear the dress whites anymore. You could go back to your trademark black leather outfits."

Verna smiled at him like she had caught him with his hand in the cookie jar and asked, somewhat sarcastically, "Would that be for me... or for you?"

"Ummm... for both of us!" he said. Verna just shook her head and looked out the window. After a moment or two he whispered gently in her ear, "Penny for your thoughts."

"Oh, I was just thinking of the last known encounter with a descendant of the Nephilim here on Earth. It took a young boy named David and his slingshot to eliminate their champion, Goliath. Now, it may take a man named David and a Cestris fighter to eliminate the next Nephilim champion."

Randall squeezed her and said, "If a young boy named David was a surprise to them back then, they're really going to be in for a surprise when they meet Rocket Babe."

Verna leaned back into him firmly, looked up at the night sky again and said, "God help us all."

Glossary Of Terms

CAG Commander Air Group

DSSF Deep Space Strike Force

EVA Extra vehicular activity

FIDO Flight Dynamics Officer

Guidance Guidance Officer

Houston Flight Mission Control Center Houston Texas

INCO Integrated Communications Officer

LGM Little grey man

LPS Launch Processing System

NASA National Aeronautics and Space Administration

Safety Console Safety Coordinator

U.S.(S.D.F) United States Space Defense Force

Shepard Flight Control Center for space station launch operations

Surgeon Flight Surgeon

SRN Space Radar Network

STM Support Test Manager

RTG Radioisotope thermoelectric generator

Additional Reading and Information

We hope you have enjoyed *Rocket Babe - Dust Storm*. You can share your thoughts with the author and main character by sending your email to: vernarockets@live.com and list *Rocket Babe* in the header.

For greater detail and to learn more about the author and characters of *Rocket Babe* visit *Verna & Randy's Rockets* at: www.vernarockets.com and be sure to LIKE *Rocket Babe* on Facebook to keep up with regular updates.

Also...

Would you like to build and actually fly the rockets and ships described in *Rocket Babe*? You can! Visit the *Sirius Rocketry* website at: http://www.siriusrocketry.com/sirius00.htm today! David Miller and *Sirius Rocketry* sell model kits, parts and all the supplies to construct the U.S.S. Pandora, S.S. Cestris, Eradicator and Saturn V.

To learn more about model and hobby rocketry visit the National Association of Rocketry (NAR) website: http://www.nar.org

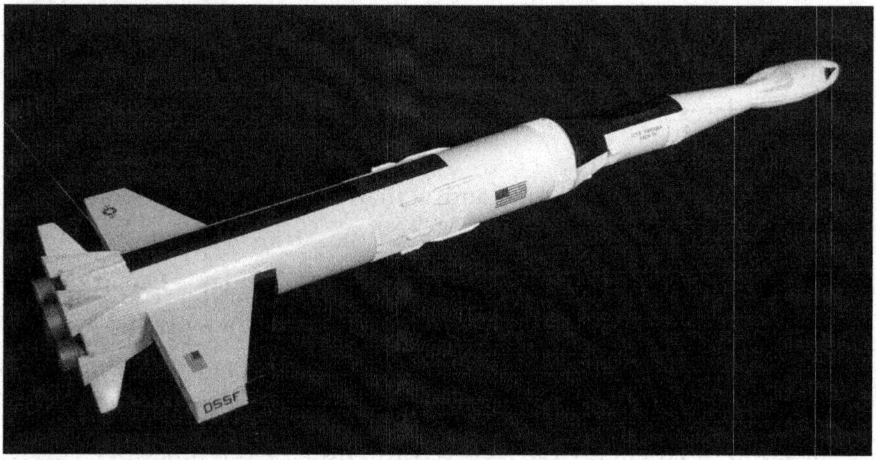
DSSF

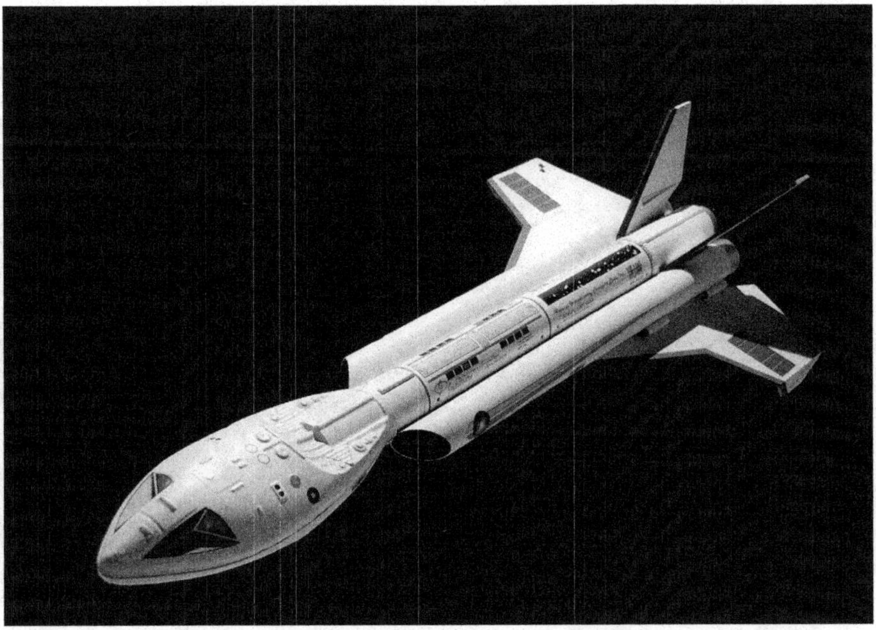

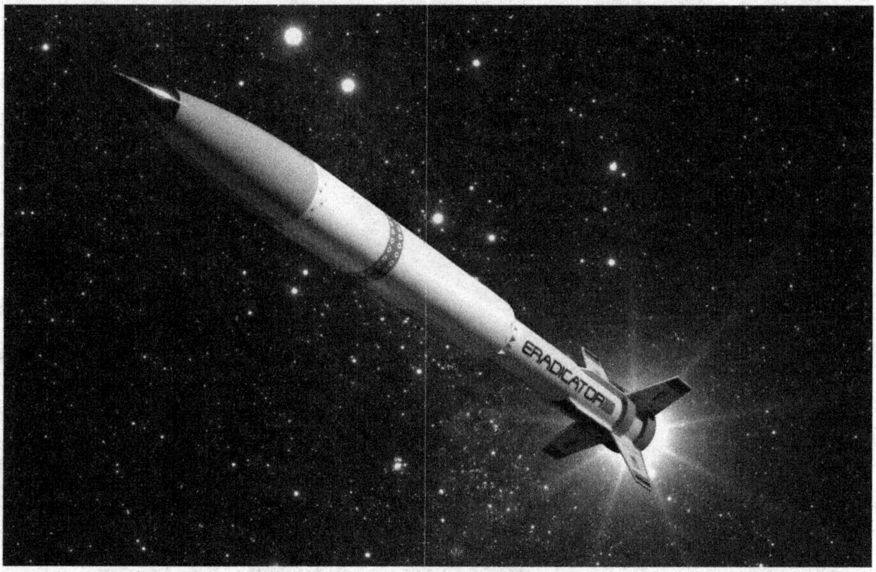
ERADICATOR

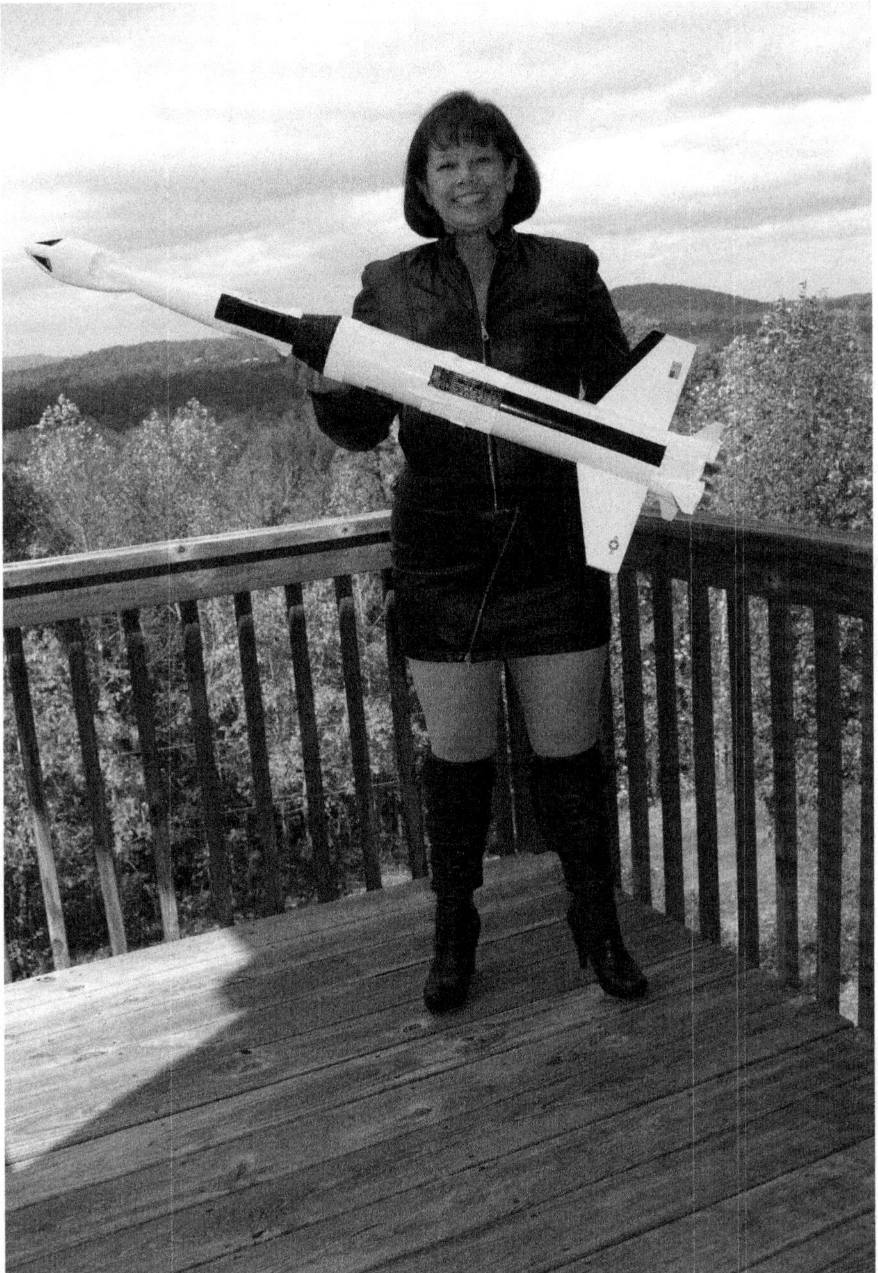